Ponckhockie Union

A NOVEL

Brent Robison

I0742584

Ponckhockie Union

Copyright © Brent Robison, 2019

Ponckhockie Union is a work of fiction. For literary effect only, it employs historical facts, real places, and a few names of actual people. Where such real-life persons, events, or locales appear, the situations, incidents, and dialogues concerning those persons, events, or locales are products of the author's imagination and are not intended to depict reality nor to change the wholly fictional nature of the work. In all other respects, any resemblance to actual persons, living or dead, or to actual events or locales, is entirely coincidental.

ISBN: 978-1-7337464-1-0
Library of Congress Control Number: 2019942327

Cover design by Bryan Maloney
Author photo by Wendy Drolma
Ponckhockie Union Church photo © Richard S. Foster, https://rsftripreporter.net/

RECITAL PUBLISHING
Woodstock, NY 12498
www.recitalpublishing.com

Recital Publishing is an imprint of the online podcast The Strange Recital.
Fiction that questions the nature of reality
www.thestrangerecital.com

CONTENTS

Acknowledgments   v

Pasts, Arising
1: Today   3
2: Heat   7
3: Legacy   19
4: Ponckhockie   25
5: Kingston   33
6: Cross   39
7: Dunne   43
8: Home   49
9: History   55
10: Battlefield   59
11: Chance   65
12: Church   69

Meantime
13: Hugh   75
14: Cate   79
15: Paul   87

Camera Obscura
16: Darkness   101
17: Lester   105
18: Breathe   113
19: Void   121

20: Desert   127

21: Cinema   137

22: Union   147

23: Confrontation   151

24: Freedom   155

In the Not-Knowing

25: Cabin   163

26: Plot   167

27: Change   171

28: Camp   175

29: Fire   181

30: Fall   183

31: Millennium   191

32: Today   199

About the Author   205

ACKNOWLEDGMENTS

My immense gratitude to the following:

Wendy and Akanksha, for their love and patience.

Dr. Stephen H. Wolinsky, PhD, whose audio recording *Waking from the Trance: A Practical Course on Developing Multidimensional Awareness* provided precepts and meditation techniques in Chapters 17, 18, and 19.

Dr. Deepak Chopra, *The Book of Secrets*, for the ideas in Chapter 22.

Sri Nisargadatta Maharaj, *I Am That* (translated by Maurice Frydman, edited by Sudhakar S. Dikshit), for threads of philosophy throughout.

The leadership and congregation of Ponckhockie Union Congregational Church, Kingston, NY, for their presence on the periphery of my imaginary edifice.

The actual Paul Auster and Siri Hustvedt, for decades of inspiration.

Wendy Drolma, Tom Newton, Carl Frankel, Val Vadeboncoeur, Samuel Claiborne, Will Nixon, and Kevin Swanwick, for their reading time and insightful comments.

PASTS, ARISING

1: TODAY

Right now the air is fresh and bright, warming after a frost. I'm grateful to need neither sweater nor jacket as I sit here on my deck. Sunshine and breeze wrestle to decide which controls the temperature. The lawn glistens, striped by long afternoon shadows of tree trunks, and occasionally the forest shivers and twinkles and yellow leaves drift singly to the ground. All sounds are a distant hum and shush—a car on the road, an airplane, rustling treetops—but then a lone birdsong, from somewhere near to my right, dips and twirls above all the sounds, like a dragonfly over a pond.

I have a story to tell, but first, I will ground myself in my own internal world of perception. This is my way.

In my leg that rests across the opposite knee, I feel the pulse of my blood, a steady beat. I see the wrinkles in the skin of my hands. This aging hulk of flesh and blood and bone is my current manifestation of self, in this here and now. Sometimes I feel closely identified with it, sometimes not. Right now this body just seems like any other random event, an arising in the field of awareness, like the birdsong a moment ago.

It doesn't feel like "me." Whatever that is.

Random arisings… like the fly that just landed, touched my finger, and flew away. Or the shadow that just crossed my page and, when I looked up, became a perfect brown oak leaf dancing its way down the air to the ground.

Or like the thoughts, images, feelings that follow one after another through my mental space, some of them carrying the label of "memory" and others the label of "imagination." Yet each is nothing more than a current circumstance, a little electrochemical flicker in the brain, happening nowhere and nowhen but here and now: Willow, New York. October 17th, 2015.

I meditate on these ideas while the story takes shape in the dark reservoir beneath.

It's entirely possible that there is no such thing as linear time: past, present, future. Maybe the apparent timeline we call a life is just a creation of the human mind. Yet, along its illusory course, strands of linked events meander and fork and intertwine like rivers seen from an airliner window.

Yesterday and today, suddenly my past has invaded my present.

Yesterday afternoon, the 16th, while my wife was working, I sat at home looking through old videotapes from over twenty years ago. My ten-year-old daughter, Chandra, is into roller skating and I wanted to show her the skate-dancers in Central Park that I had shot on video in the early nineties. I dug out my ancient Sony 8mm Handycam and shuffled through a box of poorly-labeled tapes, viewing the footage on the camera's little fold-out screen.

After several tries, I found a tape marked *Aug '94 Park* and fast-forwarded it until I saw skating footage. Tinny disco music blared out of the miniature speaker as I watched the graceful, funky dancers skating in circles. It's interesting what time will do. I had no memory of being the eye behind that camera, as if someone else had shot this scene. I watched as the camera panned across the crowd of tourists and gawkers.

Then a gesture caught my eye. The flutter of a hand. A left hand wiping sweat from a brow, a flick of wrist, an angle of elbow, a moment gone. It echoed a memory, long repressed, of an inexplicable disaster, a wrenching turn in my path.

I immediately stopped the playback and rewound the tape, back to where I'd seen the gesture. Yes. There he was. A man whose face was so bland it was easy to overlook, almost invisible. It was a face that had gradually dissolved into a blur in my memory, out of reach. But now here it was again. The face of a man I once called Double Naught, as in: no, none, a negation. A man like a black hole, who shed no light.

Two decades had passed since I saw that face. I had hoped to never see it again.

I spent the next hour looking with care through the rest of that tape and another one from the same summer. I kept my focus always on the background, the blur of passing strangers, that New York City human atmosphere that becomes almost invisible. I glimpsed him two more times, once at Bethesda Fountain and again on Central Park West.

Gradually the revelation dawned: he had been following me. Even then, a full year before we met, before the events tumbled down on my head like a building collapsing, he had been there. Watching me. Planning. The old familiar dread, gone for so long now, crept again up my spine. Is he still watching me, even now, waiting to swoop down and destroy?

That discovery itself was unsettling enough, but there was also the fact of today's date, a date inextricably connected to the man on the tape. A truly odd coincidence, except that I don't believe in mere coincidence. And then my questions were intensified even more by what happened this morning.

Around 10 a.m. my journalist friend Paul called and asked me to meet him at the mortuary in Woodstock, and to be prepared to view a corpse. He wouldn't say more. I left immediately and drove the five miles into town, dreading what might be in store. Paul and I had met in the nineties during that same difficult period that was already nagging at my mind. Even though we still see each other occasionally, I had the inexplicable sense that his call was related to those long-gone times.

October 16th and 17th: the dates of the burning of Kingston and the surrender at Saratoga during the Revolutionary War, dates that once ruled all my thoughts, that summer twenty years ago when I was so irrationally immersed in that little slice of American history. The year of change, the year that marked the end of one self, the beginning of another.

In the chilly prep room of Lasher Funeral Home, the mortician pulled back a sheet and I saw an elderly man with long, tangled gray hair and beard. For a moment I was blank, then I recognized him: this was a man who wandered the streets of Woodstock, silent but often smiling. His sole occupation seemed to be painting graceful Sanskrit symbols—*Om* and *Om Mani Padme Hum*—on rocks, boards, driftwood, then giving the pieces away to whomever took his fancy. He had given more than one to my wife—they decorate our front porch and a couple of window sills—and she had told me he was very sweet to her. Among the several eccentric street folk of Woodstock, he was the most lovable. His death from a heart attack was a sad event for our town, yes… but I never knew his name or where he lived and had never had any direct contact with him. Why was Paul showing me his body?

I have an answer. But the answer requires a long, convoluted tale—especially in light of what I found yesterday afternoon. Synchronicity carries meaning. Yesterday the man on tape, today the dead man—the two of them forever connected in a long-past mystery, unsolved.

I'll never know the whole truth. But now, I can't help it, I have to look back. Two specters from my past suddenly here again, on these dates. I have to go over the story once more, once more, as if maybe this time it will make sense.

2: HEAT

I suppose that if I'd known what would happen later, I never would have driven upstate that long-ago day. Or maybe I would have, but I wouldn't have spoken to Nils Nilsson when I did; I would have just nodded and turned away when he said hello. And even if I had spoken to him, I wouldn't have called him the next week to follow up on his offer. That was the turning point.

Or maybe it wasn't. Maybe the decisive moment was much earlier, when I first decided to make the film. But of course, all this speculation doesn't matter, because I didn't know what would happen. One never can. So I did what I did, the events tumbled after like dominoes, and I landed in the middle of something I never could have imagined, with no way out. By the time it was all over, my life had been altered forever.

To this day, there are still far more questions than answers about what was going on that summer, but that's okay. I've grown a lot since then; I've learned to prefer the questions. And the ironic thing is that as much as I might say that I would have liked to avoid what happened, still I know that all of it was bringing me to where I am now, and I wouldn't want today to be any different.

The date it all started was July 15, 1995, a Saturday. Earlier that morning freak windstorms had inflicted massive forest damage in the Adirondacks—"blowdown" they call it, broken trunks and limbs tangled twelve feet deep in places. At the same time, a heat wave was blasting the entire eastern half of the country. I learned later that over 160 people in Chicago died as a result of the temperature that day. The New York area had a heat index of 112°. Also, the dew point was abnormally high, which meant not only that the humidity was nearly unbearable, but also that air conditioners, designed for a specific dew point, couldn't do their job. Over the next two weeks, some days set all-time records of power usage. More people died.

On that Saturday, I was driving up the New York State Thruway on my way to the city of Kingston, exit 19. I had left my office in Jersey City around 1:00, intending to arrive a little early for my 3 p.m. appointment with a Mr. Randall O'Brien, owner of one of the oldest houses in Kingston. I wanted to feature his house, maybe even him and his family as well, in a film I was planning to make. At this stage the film was officially just speculation, with strong interest from the State University of New York, but no contract. And I wanted to eventually sell it to PBS. It was to be a historical documentary—a series actually—about the beginnings of New York, the story of its transformation from a British colony into a state, one state in a new young nation of states, united. I was attracted to the fact that it was not general knowledge that Kingston was New York's first capital; it had played a brief but important role in the drama, and gotten burned in the process. I was going to shed some light on those facts, among others.

I also had a secret agenda, one that I never mentioned to potential funding sources, who tended to be politically conservative. I wanted to promote a subtle revisionist history, take the official record out of the hands of the moneyed elite and put it where it belongs: with ordinary citizens. I had read Howard Zinn's *A People's History of the United States*. I was a Zinn man but I would smile and pretend I wasn't, and people would give me money. Then I would make the movie I wanted to make and they always loved it, never realizing the subtle ways I was undermining their corporate gospel. There was never much profit in this, but I was proud to have succeeded several times, and I was hopeful this one would go the same way.

But the film never got made. It started as another typical idea, one of my many dreams, that my wife and business partner, Cate, called "lovely, insubstantial schemes" as she blamed them for all our financial struggles. But this one ended far differently from the ones that had come before, and the fact that our marriage ended along with it is only a small part of the damage done, the blowdown, of that summer.

On the afternoon that my adventure began, I was at the usual stage of information gathering, preliminary interviews, location scouting. In those days I always carried with me a small video camera, and I had just bought a Sony model, the first of the new breed of all-digital camcorders using Mini-DV tape. That meant I got surprisingly good quality with handheld mobility, plus the convenience of quickly dumping the footage to a computer in my office and making rough cuts for planning purposes. It was the perfect note-taking camera for a dinosaur like me who always wanted to do the "real" production on film. Thirty-five millimeter if the budget could handle it. Film—that old-fashioned analog stuff with sprocket holes and a thin coating of light-sensitive chemistry that made such beautiful pictures, pictures with subtlety and truth that the magnetics and electronics of video could never capture. At least, not in those days, before HD.

But of course, while I dreamed of warmly lit, gracefully composed motion pictures, the world was passing me by with flashy bytes and sparkling pixels. My company—I say "company" despite the fact that it was me, alone, doing most of the work—had already done a couple of video productions for paying clients, with not a single foot of celluloid to be seen. I was being dragged into digital video because—*Don't you get it?* the voices of reason said—it was cost-effective.

Still, for this historical series, it seemed justified, even necessary, to choose the right medium. I really, really wanted to make a film, not a video. I was prepared to fight, to fight my wife, to hold on to artistic integrity. But it all came to naught. On the seat at my side was the bag that held the camera about which I had this paradoxical mix of feelings: such a fun, efficient little marvel; such a threat to all I held dear.

I drove and sweated. I sweated because, when I bought my little Hyundai—the cheapest car in America the previous year—I had opted for the most basic model. No air conditioning. Such was my financial condition. But I made that decision also because I was typically not much bothered by heat, even in the intense grimy humidity of New York City summers. I surrender to sweat, I let the glistening film cover my body, and I go about doing the things I want to do. I'm grateful I do not suffer. Sweat forms on my upper lip under my mustache, in the crease of my neck under my beard. I wipe it away; that's all.

Today, right now, two decades after the events of that July, here on the hidden bank of the Little Beaver Kill in Willow, the weather is perfect, the temperature cool, the breeze gentle, and the hot, dirty city far away and forgotten.

But on that day, not even my standard cooling method (the one my father had made the same joke about every summer of my childhood, varying it only to fit the numbers to the situation: "Got the 4-60 System on," he'd announce with a grin as if we'd never heard it before, "4 windows open, 60 miles an hour")—not even the constant 75 mile-per-hour breeze from my open windows could disguise the fact that it was hot, damned hot.

The window roar was drowning the music from my tape

deck and I hated struggling to hear my favorite album. Better to shut it off. Leonard Cohen had just started on the song "Anthem" and was telling me to dwell on neither the past nor the future when I ejected the tape with a brutal clunk. I told myself there was a sort of music in the white noise of the Thruway. Listen for it.

Between exits 17 and 18, I came suddenly upon traffic stopped dead across both northbound lanes, a few cars even parked on the shoulder. The obstruction was too far ahead to be seen. I was in the fast lane, and the feeling of forward motion inexplicably halted was disorienting; the Thruway was not a place for standing still. Some people just stayed in their cars, air conditioners blasting. Others got out, stood talking in small groups, or tried to see ahead, even by climbing on the roofs of their vehicles. I watched. Here was one of the things I've always loved about New Yorkers (and I've been to enough other places to know it's not universal): they can make a social event out of anything. There's no such thing as a stranger when you're all in a bind together. Although I've been among them since the day I was born, I've always felt a bit outside that way of thinking, a bit withholding, withdrawn, reticent about self-disclosure. But I love the way these garrulous, crusty, straight-talking neighbors of mine can draw me out.

Minutes crawled by. Two police cars made their way up the shoulder, weaving between parked cars, to get to the scene ahead. I overheard conversations; someone said an ambulance had gone by earlier. I sat in my car. There was nothing on the radio about the blockage. Without motion, the open window was no help; I couldn't even hang my arm out because any contact with metal would mean a serious burn. I oozed; my shirt stuck to the seat. I opened the door and stood up, hoping to catch a stir in the torpid air.

"Killer hot day, eh?" I heard from behind.

I turned to see a tall skinny guy in a short-sleeved yellow

shirt and khaki slacks approaching from one of the cars behind me. I guessed he was older than me, fifty-ish. He wore thick glasses and several pens in his shirt pocket. Strands of thin blond hair were sweat-plastered across his balding dome. "Any idea what's going on?"

"Nah, I don't have a clue," I said. "Nothin' on the radio."

"Got a long trip ahead?" He swabbed moisture from his brow with a bare hand and wiped it on his pants. In addition to the big dark circles in his armpits, his shirt was showing small wet spots here and there, growing as I watched.

"Just trying to get to Kingston; what... 20 miles? Gonna be late for an appointment now." I wasn't sure I wanted a conversation with this stranger, but there seemed to be nothing else to do. "How about you?"

"Going home. Little nowhere place called Quaker Springs, Saratoga County. Beautiful there. Peaceful." His shoulders were rounded, his shoes in a V, toes out, and his hands hung unnaturally still at his sides. "I've been at a conference in the big city for a couple of days. Now I'm just wanting to relax at home in the country, y'know? But... patience is a virtue, they say."

We stared ahead for few seconds. I felt uncomfortable, as I often do when it seems that small talk is required. I surrendered to the pressure. "What kind of conference?"

"A.L.A.—American Library Association. I'm a librarian. But my name isn't Marian, ha ha." His tall body made a sudden weaving motion, a little stationary dance. His fingers flared in front of him, then all went stock still again. I assumed the little grimace on the lower half of his face was a smile at his own lame joke. He jabbed a thumb toward my car. "I see by your license plates you're from New Jersey. What brings you to Kingston?"

It was not in my nature to be very glib about my work, especially in the beginning stages. "Oh, just some historical research— Revolutionary War stuff."

Behind the thick lenses, his eyes widened. "Really? Please say more."

I found myself wondering if this guy was some kind of crank, but at the same time feeling he was likable—odd but trustworthy. An innocent. And I had nothing to hide, after all. "Well... did you know that the British burned Kingston to the ground during the Revolution?"

"Yes, I certainly did... do... I do know that. I'm kind of an American history buff myself. I gather you'll be visiting the Senate House, the old stone homes uptown, and so on?

"Well, yes, eventually. Today I'm headed down to the riverfront to an area called Ponckhockie, where they say the first house was burned."

"Oh, yes. Can't say I know much about that. But, when you're in the neighborhood, you should drop by the Ponck-hockie Union Congregational Church. Beautiful piece of architecture, one of the first uses of reinforced concrete. Dates from 1870 or so, not exactly the time-frame you're investigating, but...."

I wasn't especially interested. "I'll check it out."

We both peered north again for a few seconds, then he spoke with a rush of enthusiasm. "So if you're an expert on the Revolution, I'm sure you *must* have been to Saratoga. My house is right on the edge of the old battlefield there, the north end, near the Benedict Arnold monument. You probably know far more than I, so please, forgive any *faux pas*—Saratoga, of course, was *the* big turning point in the war. Those nasty ol' redcoats never quite recovered, and it proved to the world that America was a force to be reckoned with."

At his mention of Benedict Arnold, I felt a wall go up in myself. It was an old sore point, a long story, one that I'll tell later. My chuckle was disingenuous. "An expert? I'm definitely no expert. I don't know much at all, really. I mean, who can remember their high school history class? Not me."

"Oh, I suppose you're right." His smile slumped a bit.

I wiped a drop of sweat from my eye. I wanted to brush him off, but I was also curious about his knowledge. "I'm just beginning to study this stuff—it's actually for a film project I'm doing for SUNY. I've heard of the Battle of Saratoga but never been there."

"Tell you what...." He pulled a plastic business card holder and a pen out of his overloaded shirt pocket. "If you ever have the desire to come on up and check it out, give me a ringy-dingy. Here, I'll put my home number on the back." He hunched over the card in his right hand and scribbled with his left.

"I just may take you up on that," I said, and the truth is, I wasn't pretending. Oddball or not, maybe he was a real resource, a librarian with historical smarts and local connections. My childish touchiness about America's most famous traitor was no reason to ignore an opportunity. I leaned into the car and extracted a card from my camera bag. "Here's mine."

He spoke as he moved my card up and down, searching for focus. "And by the way— these things happened at the same time, did you know that? Vaughan's men torched Kingston—a nasty little exercise in punishment, with no strategic justification—and the very next day, Burgoyne surrendered to Gates at Saratoga, while the ruins of Kingston smoldered." My card disappeared into his bulging pocket. "I mean, no cause and effect there, I'm just saying it's quite a coincidence, don't you agree? That we meet here on the road, each with some kind of relationship to those October days way back in 1777. And speaking of burning, I *must* get back in the A.C. immediately. Nice conversing with you."

He turned abruptly and walked back the way he came, south along the shoulder. As I turned away I felt sincerely impressed with the details he'd just spouted; they echoed in my head. Plus, I'm always a sucker for that term "coincidence;" I want to look below the surface. There was more at play here than this stranger knew. Something about the fact that he had unwittingly touched a raw nerve gave the whole thing a multi-layered resonance that I found fascinating. Inside, I felt something like a smile, despite the temperature.

I looked north again, craning my neck fruitlessly, then walked over to the guardrail, squinting into the hazy distance. Nothing to see but hundreds of vehicles lined up, receding into the distance in the shimmering heat, to disappear behind a grove of trees. Across the wide grassy swale of the median, cars and trucks whizzed south, free as birds. I sat down in my car with the door still open and looked at the card in my sweaty hand. It read: Nils Nilsson, Director, Schuylerville Public Library, Schuylerville, NY. I never saw what car he was driving.

I stood again, I sat, I sweated. Those were the days before everyone had a cell phone, so our miniature city on the blacktop baked in ignorance. We had no choice; we all gave in to the mystery and let patience rule. The sun beat down through a thin white haze; the highway radiated heat. We suffered together.

Finally, after nearly an hour, traffic began to move again, and as I slowly made my way around a wide bend a mile ahead, I saw the cause. I had already guessed what had happened: a car fire. Once before, on an incredibly hot day, I had been delayed by a car ablaze in the narrow, grimy, shadowy underpass that led from the Holland Tunnel to New Jersey Routes 1 and 9. It was a surreal scene, like an urban war zone. This time, as I waited, I had pondered the irony that the main focus of my trip was fire—the burning of Kingston—and the only obstacle to its success so far was probably fire.

In the center of the median, across the guardrail, sat a minivan burnt to a cinder. Impossible to tell its original color; it was gray and black, with no windows or upholstery left, and the ground charred all around it. The guardrail was dented and leaning as though the car had crashed against it, perhaps even rolled over it, before landing and bursting into flame. It must have been a huge roaring blaze. But when I got there, there was no sign of the occupants. Had they gotten out before the explosion? Or were they burned to death in an instant? Or something in between, an even more ghastly thought—life with terrible burns.

Plus, it was a family type of car. I imagined a man driving his wife and kids upstate for a weekend in the country. I made him up in present tense, like a character in a movie: perhaps he's a busy New Yorker, overworked to make ends meet in that cruel, overpriced city, and he hasn't slept because he had deadlines to meet before he could take this tiny vacation, but the family is happy to be driving upstate, maybe to see grandparents or go fishing, and the man feels good. He smiles at his wife, he jokes with his kids. And then in the next minute he is dozing, and running off the road, and rolling, and bursting into flame. A whole family—its dreams, its potential, its legacy, its endless branching story—is over, cut short in a few seconds of hell. This is a father's responsibility. This was a man's failure as a father, a failure hidden in the very heart of apparent success. The smoking remains tell the truth: the actual man was not with his family on a sweet vacation; the actual man was at work, at the office, at his paid labor. This cremation was his choice, and he chose it by choosing his drug, his obsession, his god, and then lying to himself and those he pretended to love. His was the worst sort of betrayal.

I could say this to myself because I knew that father. He could have been me. There were so many times that I had begun to nod off after all-nighters in the editing room, cruising up this very highway toward some Catskills campground, wife and child belted in and trusting me. But Cate was always watching; she'd punch me on the shoulder, hard, and say "Ben! Pull over, we're trading places." And I'd get a nap in the passenger seat while she took over and got us to our destination safely. I remember tears jumping to my eyes that day as I felt a rush of gratitude for her strength. Without it, who knows the damage I could have done to our family?

We could have ended up like the people in the minivan, the family in my imagination, victims of someone like me. My own guilt—that was the lesson to be learned from a burning car on the edge of a highway. But then I thought again. It's also possible that, simply, there is no meaning to be found. No lesson, no fault. Perhaps the blind machinations of chance put a car with a random mechanical defect in the possession of this driver, and a whole family is dead, with nobody to blame. We are all powerless in the beautiful mindless flow of the stream, in the steady endless current of the universe.

That is, whatever universe we happen to be in. The year before, I had been studying quantum physics and super-string theory, and knew that cutting-edge science now allowed for the possibility of an endless number of simulta-neous universes, each only a slight variation of the others. It was confirmation of Borges' fiction, one of my favorite sto-ries, *The Garden of Forking Paths*, and I thought, somewhere in an alternate universe that family in the minivan continues happily on their vacation. Just like all the religious people who manufacture the myth of heaven to ease the unbearable pain of losing a loved one, couldn't I take refuge in some-thing as well?

3: LEGACY

My name is Ben Rose. The surname is an Americanization of the Russian, Rozovsky. The Rozovskys were merchants who exploited their Jewish ethnicity but had lost their religion generations back. The name was changed by my grandfather, who discovered quickly once he got his young family off the boat in 1921 that having a more American name would work in his favor. My dad seemed to have developed a complicated relationship with that decision of his father's; realizing its benefits, he never changed the name back, but he always resented both his father's acquiescence to capitalism and a nation that made such denial of heritage necessary. He was vocal about his opinions. My father was a Communist, "card-carrying" as they say. But in my view it mostly amounted to gathering with his cronies weekly and grousing about the government. His entire employment career was spent with the PATH system, Port Authority Trans Hudson, headquartered in Journal Square in Jersey City. He held every job from the bottom up, finally landing in a middle-management position that challenged his pro-labor stance so severely he could climb the ladder no further. But he couldn't afford to slide back down; he had a family to support. So he existed in the inner and outer strife of incongruence.

And he had a chip on his shoulder. It expressed itself in rigid, scowling silence—a man alone against the world. I was born, his first child, just two years after the execution of Julius and Ethel Rosenberg. That nasty madman Senator Joe

McCarthy was on his way out, but the Red Scare still had a stranglehold on the country, and my parents lived in constant fear of harassment or worse from neighbors, co-workers, bosses. I'm sure my father felt squashed down, full of impotent rage.

Dad died in April of '95, just three months before the events I'm telling about began. He died alone, apparently of heart failure, an 83-year-old curmudgeon in his Brooklyn apartment, the apartment he'd lived in ever since he and my mother split up when I was in college. We hadn't been close for many years, but we'd been cordial in occasional phone conversations, and now I couldn't quite accept that I would never hear that gruff voice again. He was suddenly, permanently gone: an acceptable absence turned suddenly unacceptable. After three months, I was still at that stage where the feeling would rush over me at any time of day or night, absolutely unexpected, of utter aloneness, of being a man at the edge of an abyss, the next in line to drop into blackness. As long as he was alive, I had been somehow protected, still a child.

Despite spending most of his life in Jersey City, going to school there, raising a family, my father had always felt himself to be a New York City man through and through. After the age of fifty, he had methodically walked every block of every street in Manhattan, working his way from Battery Park to the top of Harlem. It took him over twenty years, and by the time he was finished, he had an almost mystical air about him whenever the topic of conversation turned to the city itself, as if he had gone to a deep inner place of understanding that most of us would never attain. He marked his progress with a pencil line on an old map, nothing more. He did not record the experience in any way, not a photograph nor a note—a choice I could never understand. Still I feel that his New York walk is the best of the legacies he left me, the one for which I am most grateful.

Another legacy, rather more twisted, is my love-hate relationship with politics. As thoroughly secular as our home was, nevertheless it was steeped in religion. Our God was the Left, our Satan the Right. I was tempted toward the forbidden side often, even as I knew it was mostly just a reaction to my parents. During most of my adult life, when my artsy friends would talk politics at parties, I would excuse myself, even though I agreed with the liberal views they were expressing. I just wanted to avoid the perverse devil's-advocate voice that would rise up in me, almost like vomit.

My parents, ever the iconoclasts, had never divorced, just gone their separate ways. Mom was a fellow traveler politically but was never the faithful meeting-goer, I suspect because she had a home to keep and children to raise. She did work tirelessly for leftist candidates whenever election season rolled around. Mom came from an Italian family of professed anarchists and lapsed Catholics, who hung photos of Sacco and Vanzetti on their parlor walls. When Dad died, Mom was living in Florida near my younger sister Emma and her husband and four kids—continually, Emma told me, "rabble-rousing" amongst the other senior citizens in her condo development.

In our childhood home there was an unspoken expectation that my sister and I and the other "red diaper babies" of our generation would somehow rise up and save our fucked-up country from itself. Toward my artistic leanings, my filmmaking aspirations, my mother gave cheery, if insincere, support. But my dad's attitude vacillated between head-shaking silent scorn and a false enthusiasm accompanied by the demand that I use my skills to promote the Party and its aims.

Ha! Me, a commie propagandist. Not a chance. Nevertheless, the lockjawed puritan that headed our family was the inescapable father of both my body and my mind. How could I not ingest the grim endurance that he exuded? How could I not breathe the air?

As Dad wished, we had his body cremated right away, and had no memorial service, just a gathering of family and a half-dozen old friends. Some I remembered and others I didn't, both men and women, "over-the-hill Bolsheviks like me" he would have called them. They showed real pleasure to see my mother again, a long-missed comrade. In Dad's honor, we did something completely illegal. We took our little procession—the stooped elderly, the harried middle-aged, the rowdy children—onto the Staten Island Ferry and gathered in a tight group at the rear railing. Everyone watched in silence as I surreptitiously dumped my father's ashes into the ferry's wake as it churned New York Harbor. Thus he was made forever one with the city he had loved. As the gray dust disappeared in the foam and drifted away on the breeze, we all looked at each other, smiled as if a solemn spell had broken, and that was the end of it. The rest of the trip across and back was full of chatting, reminiscences, running children.

There's one more legacy that my father left me, maybe the most important one: my name. I don't mean the surname, I mean the first and middle. I go by Ben, and of course most people assume it is short for Benjamin. But on my birth certificate it reads: Benedict Arnold Rose. I bear the name of the most famous traitor in American history.

The man whose name is synonymous with treason was one of my father's heroes. At the root of this juvenile contrariness was the attitude he developed toward the U.S. Army during the years he served in World War II. He saw what he believed to be elitist privilege for officers and brutal mistreatment of the common soldier. So when he learned that Benedict Arnold's treachery was motivated by resentment for unjust treatment by the army, by its bosses, my father formed a bond with him across the centuries. It seemed preposterous to me, even as a teenager, and I rejected the whole edifice. I refused to study my namesake, knew only of his cowardly attempt to hand West Point over to the British, betraying the trust of George Washington and the righteous American cause. I made sure I was absent on the day he was discussed in high school American History class. I hated the mixture of petulance and pride that my father displayed when he occasionally brought up the subject, and I went about denying its effect on me. I was always simply Ben. If an official signature was required, I allowed myself to become Benedict A. Rose, and I cringed as I signed it.

My sister was named after Emma Goldman, a far more reasonable selection in my opinion. Still, I chose in my adolescence to just call her E, to repudiate the entire concept of names upon which my parents had placed such importance. What power does a name have? Does it have any bearing on who we really are? I struggled to answer those questions most of my life. Today, I understand the problem so much better, but it was not an easy knowledge to gain.

So when Nils Nilsson mentioned a monument to Benedict Arnold, I pretended it meant nothing to me, when the truth is, it meant a great deal. I wanted nothing whatsoever to do with it, but at the same time, I felt an infantile craving for an answer: why on earth would there be a monument to such a scoundrel?

4: PONCKHOCKIE

I'd been to the city of Kingston a few times before, but always just on the fringes—to those generic gas stations, convenience stores, and diners that line every major highway in America. This time I was trying to keep my eyes on the streets while also following the detailed directions I'd scrawled as I spoke on the phone with Mr. O'Brien a few days earlier. I cruised down Broadway, a long drab strip of discount drug stores, print shops, ethnic eateries of various sorts, supply houses for the building trades, a hospital, anonymous retail and service businesses. There were plenty of cars on the street but few people walking; I attributed it to the heat. I felt a faint sense of alarm when I passed a towering Gothic brick structure in pitiful disrepair, clearly uninhabited, with "City Hall" on the sign out front. It stood across from the once-majestic Greek Revival columns of an aging high school, also without a soul on the grounds. Then I spotted a few huge old homes on the hillsides as the street curved under shade trees and took me down a straight, open slope toward boats and water.

This I knew was the district called "the Rondout," once a separate village, its name an English corruption of the Dutch word "reduyt," meaning redoubt, or fort. The Dutch had built primitive fortifications here in 1660, just a few years before all these vast reaches of New Amsterdam were taken over by the British and the name was changed to New York. On my left side was a row of newish attached townhouses, attempting to echo the look of the old brick struc-

25

tures lining the right side. The townhouses stood mutely in dullness—the mediocrity of the new. The original buildings were what held my attention. Some looked abandoned; some were businesses, retail shops, restaurants. I could imagine an earlier century when these were fine edifices in a bustling business district, but today, a Saturday afternoon, there was absolutely no one on the street. The whole place had the feeling of a step back in time, but not a big enough step; a sepia postcard that had tried to come to life but hadn't quite made it; a strange, hidden village where anything might be lurking in the back streets. An artists' enclave perhaps, but one where all the artists had just left town. It baked in the heat—sleepy, vacant, a little sad.

Broadway ended at Rondout Creek, where a few empty boats were docked. I caught the faintest whiff of mossy wetness in the air. Two ducks etched slow wakes in the glassy green. The creek curved away to my right into cooler shady reaches between steep overgrown hills. I turned left onto East Strand, under a highway bridge on which State Route 9W took a flying leap across the creek to the woolly heights of Port Ewen. Cars zoomed both directions over my head, part of another world, the one I had left behind when I drove down off the Kingston bluff.

I knew that East Strand was taking me along the final stretch of Rondout Creek to where it flowed into the Hudson River. That was my destination: the place where the British had landed on October 16, 1777, a piece of riverbank that was nearly uninhabited then, but was now a 200-year-old neighborhood with the whimsical, mysterious name of Ponckhockie.

With every foot of the road, I felt I was getting further from Kingston, New York, 1995. On my right was a dingy ramshackle building hung with maritime paraphernalia and a neon beer sign, apparently a working tavern. I wondered what kind of characters were inside. I passed big weedy jumbles of rusty iron, abandoned trolley cars, crumbling industrial structures from another age, dilapidated boat-yards, fences overgrown with drooping vegetation, and a handful of house-sized cylindrical oil tanks on which the dusty blue paint was peeling.

It seemed that I passed through a gateway, as if the sky grew bigger and brighter, and I entered a community of homes. To my right was a wide open vista, water, a far hazy bank, and on my left several crowded blocks ranging up a small slope backed by a forested bluff. I cruised slowly, and I heard the sound of my tires crunching gravel on the aged blacktop. Something about the light here on this hidden shore of the great river, the light and the quiet, the lazy sun-baked look of it all, transported me. I was somewhere else, in another time, maybe the Deep South, 1959. The houses were wood-frame 2-stories, some weather-beaten and ill-cared for, others tidy and trim, but none showing signs of affluence. It was a working class neighborhood, at rest on a hot summer afternoon, and I seemed to be the only per-son driving. An old black dog crossed the road without a thought of hurrying. A couple of half-dressed kids looked up from whatever they were doing on the steps of a rambling wooden stoop. A young woman in shorts with a bandana tied over her hair turned into the door of a tiny grocery. A man with his head under the hood of a weathered 70's-vin-tage Oldsmobile didn't look up at all.

The place seemed perfectly matched with its name. Ponckhockie was a word used by the Lenni-Lenape tribe, the long-gone natives of this region, to mean "dust land" or "land of ashes." Some texts claim the word suggests gun-powder, others a place of death or burial. Its almost comical sound to my American ears, accompanied by fleeting mental images of skinny punk rockers waltzing with padded hockey players, added a welcome gloss of surreal nonsense on the surface of all this grave history.

At first I just randomly turned corners, eyes roving, basking in the atmosphere of timelessness, until I remembered how late I was for my appointment with Randall O'Brien. The streets were well-enough marked and soon I pulled to a stop in front of his home, a recognized historical site known as the Yeoman House.

An unpretentious stone structure clearly older than most of the neighborhood, it stood at the foot of the tree-covered hill that formed the backdrop of Ponckhockie. This house, built in about 1742 by one Moses Yeoman, was reputed to be the first building burned when the British raided that October day in 1777. Yeoman was in the Continental Army, stationed elsewhere, when the enemy landed just a quarter mile from his home. The story was that the redcoats were moving quickly, advancing toward Kingston proper; they put the torch to Yeoman's home, but it had only begun to burn when they left it behind. A black woman, maybe a slave, hiding in the nearby cornstalks, was able to extinguish the fire before much damage was done.

I had no idea how many previous owners had made changes to the house, but it still had a charm that I assumed, with near-zero knowledge of vernacular architecture, must come from its original Dutch Colonial details. I knew that the O'Briens, recently relocated from Manhattan with the intent of raising their two small children in a gentler atmosphere, had purchased the place with visions of careful, faithful restoration.

My hope was to get O'Brien or his wife to tell the story of their home on camera, then bring it to life in the editing room with shots of details in the house, views of the river and the road the British took, inter-cut with period artwork, etchings, early photos of the area, whatever historical material I could find. But I had to meet the family first to get a sense of whether they were willing or able to participate.

One tale that I had read, and I wondered if the O'Briens

might know, was of several Dutchmen working in the tall-grass flats at the edge of the river when the British landed. Suddenly a band of redcoats was upon them, and the work-men turned and ran for their lives toward higher ground, never looking behind them for fear of what they'd see. In the meadow lay a long-handled rake left behind from sum-mer hay-making, and one of the fleeing men stepped on its upright tines. The handle flew up in an arc behind him and whacked him solidly on the back of the head. Certain that a "Britisher" was right on his heels, he stopped short, threw up his hands in surrender, and shouted (as reported by the writer of this account), "O, mein Cot! O, mein Cot! I kiv up. Hoorah for King Shorge!" But the enemy soldiers were nowhere near, and the Dutchman's sudden Loyalist conver-sion, to both his chagrin and his gratitude, was known only to one of his companions running at his side.

I never knew whether such anecdotes would end up in the finished work, but hearing them told always helped me. It would build a foundation of personal connection, of empathetic links across the years to people once like us, now long dead.

In preliminary interviews, and often during actual pro-duction, I always counted on learning bits of obscure knowledge, unexpected human interest minutiae, new twists that could be developed like a detective's clues into fresh ways of telling the story, surprising glimpses of the world through windows never seen before. A type of histor-ical truth that's deeper than the movements of armies or the machinations of the elite—the kind of story I thought maybe Howard Zinn would tell.

Reconstruction of the past always needs flashes of inspi-ration; we get at the biggest truths by crafting new, small truths. And, with a little coaxing, helpful insights always came tumbling out of the ordinary people whose stories I was investigating—these personalities whose uniqueness is the very stuff of my art; these regular folk who, though they never would have made such a claim, were full creative collaborators on my films. At least, that is, on the best of my films, the few memorable ones.

Camera bag on my shoulder, I knocked on the door of the Yeoman House. There was no answer. I could hear insects buzzing in the foliage on the hill behind. The house was silent, no car at the curb. I was an hour late. Apparently they had had someplace to go and had decided not to wait, and I couldn't blame them. I felt frustrated; it was no small task to get up here from the city, but I had no choice but to try and set the whole thing up again later. And hope O'Brien was a forgiving sort.

I also remember feeling a distinct unease. Things just seemed generally wrong, out of whack. Never very good at trusting my intuition, I blamed the heat, the long wait on the highway, my wrinkled shirt. And one more thing—I knew that Cate would not be happy to learn I had spent my Saturday afternoon, hours better dedicated to the family, so unproductively. And on a project she didn't approve of in the first place.

I decided to salvage some of the trip by shooting shots of the outside of the house as well as some of the other key locations in Kingston. It's not great etiquette to photograph someone's home when they're not present, but I did it anyway, striding around, crouching, catching several quick angles plus a view out toward the river.

Just as I was getting back in my car, I remembered Nilsson's suggestion that I should see an old church. I cruised a couple of blocks until I saw it, sandwiched on a narrow lot between homes: the Ponckhockie Union Congregational Church. It looked a bit tired, but its multi-shaded browns and grays in symmetric patterns and its pencil-stub dome gave it just enough strange beauty to entice me to take a closer look. At first glance, its walls seemed ancient, crumbling with age, but then I remembered Nilsson had said it had been built of concrete. As I approached the small set of steps leading from the sidewalk to the worn double doors, three people came out, engaged in conversation. They immediately looked up toward the roof of the church and one of the men spoke.

"So you can only imagine what a different flavor would exist in the neighborhood if our original 220-foot steeple had been able to survive. But such was the knowledge of cement construction in those days." His accent was distinctly British.

The man and woman, tourists I gathered, thanked their guide for his time and his knowledge and walked away, nodding at me as they passed.

His light blue eyes landed on me. "Hello," he said. "Are you interested in a tour of the church?"

I didn't want to get sidetracked now; I had too many other things to get done this afternoon. I put up a hand. "No, thanks. I was really just taking a quick look at the outside. Maybe I could come back another time."

"That would be just fine. I'll be here. I'm the caretaker, Lester Spanda. Call me Les." He gave me a wide grin and reached out a broad meaty hand. As I shook it, a vague sensation began to dawn in me that I had met this man before. I couldn't grasp any specific memory, so I just thanked him and walked back to my car. Then I headed back the way I came, out of Ponckhockie.

That day, I had no clue how much time I would soon be spending there, nor under what incredible circumstances.

5: KINGSTON

On my way back up Broadway, I stopped at a fast-food place to pee, get a cold soda, and use the pay phone in the entryway. First I called my office to see if there was a message on the answering machine from O'Brien. Nothing. Then I called the O'Brien home and their machine picked up, a woman's cheerful voice: "If you want to leave a message for Randy, Bridget, Emily, or Ethan, please speak after the beep." I briefly apologized for missing them due to a traffic backup on the Thruway and said I'd call again next week to set up another appointment. Then I dialed my home number, feeling faint dread about speaking with Cate. Her plan had been to keep Ava inside for the afternoon, maybe invite a playmate over, to avoid the heat outside. But there was no answer. I wasn't going to be later than she expected, so I wasn't even sure why I had called. I quickly hung up before the machine clicked on. I was feeling drained, grumpy, maybe a little lonely.

I checked my map of Kingston, then followed signs for the Stockade District. This was a part of town where I knew I'd be spending a lot of time as this project developed, since this is where all the action was: the "government on the run" and the giant conflagration. I mainly just wanted to look around a bit, get my bearings, then dedicate several full days during the coming month to exploring the place.

Although I was distracted by wondering what Cate and Ava were doing, I found my way to Main Street. This part of Kingston, "uptown," was definitely more populated, more in the world, than the riverfront had been. Cars were on the street and a few people were walking despite the heat. This was clearly a business district, so I knew it would be busier on a weekday. I passed an ill-conceived chrome and glass cube of a building, apparently the Ulster County offices, then grabbed a parking spot across the street from a beautiful old churchyard. A graceful white steeple soared above the solid stone construction, and on the lawn, a statue of a flag-bearing woman was flanked by worn gravestones standing tilted and straight. This was a place I had to see more closely.

As I got out of the car, I realized I was parked in front of a florist shop, and on impulse, decided to go in and get Cate a bouquet of something, maybe some wildflowers. I dealt with a pleasant man in the shop, who told me the Dutch Reformed Church opposite was the burial place of George Clinton, New York's first governor, and that his monument was to the left of the main entrance.

I put the flowers in the car and picked up my bag. I hadn't called ahead for permission to intrude with a camera, so I stayed on the sidewalk outside a black metal fence that fortunately was only waist high. I took several video shots of the church and graves, from different angles. I found the Clinton monument dull, an elongated pyramid with a faux torch on top. He might be an important character in the story I was just beginning to tell, but the monument gave me no information. I moved on. My zoom lens let me see more than my eyes could have seen, like the expressionless bronze face of the statue called "Daughter of the 120th Infantry New York Volunteers," close-up. This was a Civil War monument, not my chosen topic, and anyway, I wondered, why are heroic statues always so grim, so thoroughly not-alive? More compelling to me were the graves, the final resting places of ordinary citizens from another age, and the weathered, nearly obscured inscriptions that gave the merest facts, the names and dates—full lives reduced to the simplest of summaries, carved in curiously wrought script, fading with every year, soon to be completely lost.

As I panned the neighborhood with my camera, a plaque caught my eye. It was on the Burgevin Building, which housed the florist shop. It claimed that this corner, Fair Street and Main, was the site of the original blockhouse of the old stockade. That was history that was outside the scope of the film I was making, but I had read about it. The stockade was built by the Dutch in the late 1650s when Kingston was called Wiltwyck, or "savage district." The natives were not happy that these foreigners were taking the land, so this became a walled-in encampment as well as a village.

With a little guidance by the florist, I set off walking a circuitous route through the streets of the Stockade District. I took shots of the Ulster County Courthouse, which housed the New York Congress for a few months in early 1777 after it fled north from British-occupied Manhattan. The delegates, led by John Jay, met here to craft the first State Constitution, which resulted mid-year in the election of Brigadier General Clinton as the first Governor.

I grabbed views of all four corners of John and Crown streets, where the original stone houses still stand, houses gutted by fire when the British swept through.

I shot several angles of the Senate House, its adjacent museum, and the trim, shady grounds. The Senate House was the home of Abraham VanGaasbeck, who offered a meeting room to the new government when the State Supreme Court's first session in the Courthouse meant that the Legislature had to move elsewhere. The much larger Assembly met in a local tavern, a site I couldn't find, but the Senate met in VanGaasbeck's home until the British raided and the young government fled once again.

As I alternately looked through my viewfinder and

walked to each new site, my vision seemed to grow more and more overlaid with imaginary scenes like projected movies of earlier centuries. Cars and people bustled about among the buildings that sported twentieth-century skins over their older skeletons, but I felt removed. I wondered if I was fading into transparency, more ghost than human, like the other ghosts on these grounds, in these buildings, invisible and forgotten to all the present-day mortals engaged in their lives in the Now.

Back at my car, I stared at the cemetery. I was thinking about where I was, the when and the where, which was: 1995, the intersection of Fair Street and Main, in Kingston, first capital of New York State—at the site of the old stockade, built by struggling men and women to protect themselves from the "savages." But that was Then and this was Now, a time when Kingston had become, relatively speaking, a super-metropolis, unimaginable to the people who lived here when the British burned it down in 1777. And even more unimaginable in those older, rougher days of pioneering, of scraping a farm and a community of farms out of the wilderness and living in a tense balance with the natives, who probably wouldn't have made a stockade necessary at all if it weren't for arrogant European superiority—the racism of the white-faced, blue-eyed blondes who invaded and colonized this place.

There across the street were the crumbling, weathered, little headstones, ancient and alien, one with a skull and crossbones above the name and a nearly illegible notation, possibly Dutch, "Hier Leight..."—meaning, I assume, Here Lies the body of someone like me, another person with a complex life, a life as important as mine, who is now permanently gone from the world, gone without a trace and without having made a detectable impact on the universe, as if he had never existed at all.

Unless of course he left children who in turn left children and so on, such that this nameless Dutchman actually did have a tremendous impact on the world, on his future that is my present, because his descendants may be all around me when I walk down the street, may speak to me in service jobs, may affect my life in any kind of subtle way, ways I can only try to imagine. The invisible dead Dutchman lives on. And on and on. But is also gone, forever gone, just as I—unimaginable reality—will be someday. Gone but living on in the form of my children and grandchildren and so on until all memory of me recedes so far into the past that finally I am truly, completely gone. Vanished.

6: CROSS

Now, with six decades on this planet behind me, I've let go of so many self-limiting ideas. But in 1995 I was forty, an age that, it seemed to me at the time, should have meant mature self-assuredness and material success, neither of which I possessed. On paper, it all looked good: I was self-employed in an interesting field; I had been married seven years to an attractive woman and had an adorable four-year-old daughter; I lived in a condo on the Hudson River, had two cars, a cute Cairn terrier, and a handful of smart, creative friends.

The truth is, things were not working out well. Cate and I had been fighting a lot lately, and at the root of it was the cliche I hated to admit: money. Our business was really not pulling its weight, and when I say "our business," it's really just a euphemism for "my business." Except, of course, when it was profitable, then it was "her business." We had started our production company two years before we got married, so it had had a nine-year run, more than enough time, in her view, to be a great success: fortune, fame, no worries. Instead, we operated out of two small rooms in an industrial building in a slum neighborhood, we barely covered our bills every month, and we had already surrendered, after exhausting every other option, to the necessity of sending our kindergarten-aged daughter into the maw of the Jersey City public school system.

Cate's full name was Catherine Anne Cross, "two saints and their symbol," she said. She came from a prominent central New Jersey family, generations of Catholic lawyers. A rebellious streak sent her in the direction of the arts and she became a skilled graphic designer. We met when I hired her to design some animation sequences in the first film of the educational series that launched our business, and in fact carried through our first two years. It was called "From Knights to Masons: the Legacy of the Templars, Alchemists, and Rosicrucians."

Together, we fell down a rabbit hole of ancient mystery and modern romance.

One of our research sources was the 1677 alchemical masterpiece *Mutus Liber*, or "Silent Book," which is a series of mostly wordless illustrations by someone called "Altus." Cate borrowed its visual style for some of our film graphics. The densely symbolic images show a man and a woman laboring together through a series of mysterious activities: gathering morning dew on bedsheets, wringing out the liquid, distilling it, mixing its components in various combinations... but why?

Because, we learned, dew stands for dreams. Dreams also arrive in the night and, come morning, must be delicately captured and analyzed. Dreams are the *materia prima*, the lead-like raw material that must be worked with to advance toward philosophical gold. In other words, enlightenment: beyond lucid dreaming into full astral travel, even triumph over death.

Rose, I discovered, is a pun on the Latin word for dew, *ros*. So... rose = dew = dreams = astral travel = eternal life! Everywhere in the ancient texts are illustrations of roses.

The Chymical Wedding of Christian Rosenkreutz, 1459 was a book that actually appeared in 1616 and chronicles (or fictionally invents) the mythical character who founded Rosicrucianism—where Rose and Cross come together as the symbol of a secret society of Christian mystics and magicians whose existence stretched backward in time to the Knights Templar of the Crusades. And then subsequently, forward in time to the foundations of Freemasonry, with its secret rites and rituals that some writers claim are in use today by the shadowy power-elite who actually rule the world.

But on the other hand... no sooner was *The Chymical Wedding of Christian Rosenkreutz* anonymously published than a guy named Andreae claimed to be its author and famously called it a "ludibrium"—a plaything or a trivial game. In other words, a fiction. A hoax.

Did he give it that label to cover up an actual secret cult of immortal mystics? Or did his silly confabulation accidentally create a new reality in the superstitious minds of foolish humans, and roll on down through the ages to us, as if it were actually meaningful? Which of course would make it actually meaningful, by its sheer momentum.

Cate and I reveled in this stuff. Do ancient esoteric texts have some strange erotic power? We laughed, we found reasons to work late, we touched each other too much. We joked about having our own "chymical wedding"—instead of the mystical marriage of soul and spirit, we wanted the merging of flesh. Before a month was gone we found ourselves in bed together, even discussing business partnership. And our union seemed cemented by fate with the serendipitous creation of a business name that mirrored the work we had begun, the work that carried us through our first two years: Rose-Cross Productions. She crafted an elegant logo based on medieval Rosicrucian imagery but streamlined, both contemporary and esoteric. The computer revolution in commercial art was just beginning. She jumped in and mastered the digital tools right away, and, between the two of us, she was always the leader regarding current technology.

Cate was slim and athletic with auburn hair usually kept boyishly short, for no fuss. I was attracted to her agile mind and ready laugh, and, I confess, to a convoluted undercurrent of dark passion that would show itself sometimes as a sardonic lift of one corner of her mouth, other times as dish-breaking rage, and still other times as full-on erotic ecstasy.

Our wedding day was truly one of the happiest of my life, despite its location. It took place at her parents' lavish home in the green, hidden part of New Jersey. They spared no expense. In the years after that, we tried and mostly suc-ceeded at staying out from under their influence. Early on, Cate made it clear that our financial struggles were to be our own, the history of *our* family, not hers, and I loved her for that. But life can be exhausting, and parenthood shakes up the deepest of romantic convictions. We were worn down by the struggle to stay afloat, and I was anticipating that any day now she might suggest that we accept her parents' standing offer for help. I was dreading that, because to be beholden to those people was the last thing I wanted. I say "those people" because they were a dynasty of ruthless cor-porate attorneys married to ladies who lunch, and I couldn't stand them. Cate's father and two brothers patronized me in the worst way and I knew that as they teed up on the sev-enth hole or puffed on their Cuban cigars at the club, they wagged their heads and sighed *tsk-tsk* about poor Cate mar-rying such a loser.

Fuck 'em.

7: DUNNE

As I sped south on the Thruway that hot July day, the shadows grew long from the lowering sun on my right. I was just approaching the New Jersey border, preparing to exit onto Route 17, when, as if out of nowhere, a moment flooded from the reservoir of memory into my consciousness. It was some twenty years earlier, in the pink glow of dawn, on a rugged, piney plateau in the wilderness of Utah, and I was shaking the hand of a man who I was almost certain was the same man I had just met, the man at the church who called himself Lester Spanda. That handshake and the days that followed it were imprinted on my synapses because, from a visual point of view if nothing else (and there was much more than that), they stood in sharp contrast to the rest of my young life.

It had been the summer of 1975. I was a film student at NYU and had fallen in love with a girl in the Sociology department, Amy Bennett. She was from Utah, a Mormon who was doing a bit of exploring outside the rules of her religion, reveling in the eye-opening chaos of New York City. She had an opportunity for a short work-study experience with a Utah program that was getting good results taking troubled teens on long therapeutic camping trips into the desert. She invited me to come along, and I volunteered to use my newly purchased prize piece of hardware, a sixteen-millimeter Bolex camera, to document the excursion if the program would pay for the film stock and processing.

So I found myself in Provo, Utah, barely twenty, the age

43

that most Mormon boys are on a "mission" to preach their gospel. It was clear that Amy's parents didn't see me, a Jew from New Jersey, as the ideal mate for their daughter, and for the couple of nights we spent at their house, we pretended we had never touched one another, and we slept in different rooms. What a relief it was to get out on the highway, heading to the fabulous deserts that Utah is known for.

Amy and I, three adult leaders, and eleven teenagers with various degrees of bad attitude caravanned in a pickup and two vans through wilderness like nothing I had seen before: vast stretches of empty crumpled land broken by sudden ragged upthrusts of stone and distant snowy peaks. We snaked up through sweeps of rippled sandstone to a high, green plateau dotted with occasional ranch buildings, passed through a tiny hamlet, and continued into a pristine forest of tall evergreens. We were told this was Boulder Mountain, our launch point. By this time it was late afternoon, and our immediate goal was simply to unload, hike a short distance, and set up our first overnight camp. We walked no more than a mile through the fresh-scented silence of the pine woods and came out on a brushy flat area that seemed to overlook the entire earth. Below was a limitless vista of twisted canyons, jutting cliffs, jagged ridgelines, and sprawling emptiness, all turning golden in the slant of the sun. We made camp as the light fell to blue then black, built a fire, cooked burgers, and sat up late around the blaze, everyone excited about what was to come the next morning, when the trip really started.

That following dawn was when I met Jack Dunne. He had arrived silently in the dark morning hours, our desert survivalist expert, our guide, ready to begin the excursion with us. He shook the hand of every one of us and looked us in the eye as he learned our names. He was a solidly-built, pale-skinned Englishman with short strawberry-blonde hair and a broad face on the plain side of handsome, a pleasant everyman face wearing an open, friendly smile.

It was later, as we walked and rested together, that I learned who he really was. Or, rather, who he said he was. I remember thinking at the time that I didn't know whether to believe him because if his stories were true, why would he talk about it to a bunch of kids? He talked too much. He loved to hear himself talk.

Jack Dunne was a mercenary soldier. He said he was a well-known expert in everything military—weapons, explosives, survival, covert operations. He was a master marksman, a gun smuggler, even a forger. He had been in Vietnam, had killed people, many people, sometimes in close combat, face to face, with a knife. He was known as "Mad Dog Dunne."

He made a point of getting to know me so that he could make this very clear: he did not want to appear in my film. He wanted no photos of himself. He said this with the kind of smile that meant he was deadly serious. The strange thing is that at other times, I saw him pose dramatically for a couple of the kids who had brought their instamatic cameras along.

As we sat together on a boulder during a short rest stop on the third morning, Dunne told me one more thing. He said he had been recently contacted by people who "shall remain nameless," offering him the job of assassinating Yasser Arafat, Chairman of the Palestinian Liberation Organization. It was not a problem for him, practically or ethically; he knew he could accomplish the task. He was planning to take it on. Maybe this time next year he'd be sitting pretty in some fancy resort under a different name, living a life of luxury. Not that he cared about that sort of thing.

That was enough for me. I really didn't want to hear anything more from Jack Dunne. I was a peacenik, an occasional anti-Vietnam marcher, but mostly I was an artist, a dreamer, a sensitive kid who wanted to get lost in creative work and stay in denial about the kind of work Jack Dunne did—if it was even true. He was a player of mind games, if not a murderer. He disturbed me, and I avoided him for the rest of my short participation in that desert journey.

The plan Amy and I had made was that I would only stay for the first three days of the ten-day trip, then, with one of the other program leaders, I would hike out of the canyons and return to civilization. I felt that was necessary to protect my camera and the film I had shot from too much exposure to the elements, but also, I was broke. I had to get back to my job in a print shop in Hell's Kitchen. I would fly out of Salt Lake while she stayed in the desert, and we would see each other again when she returned to New York at the end of the summer.

Few things ever work out as planned. My tiny personal traumas just blended in with a general feeling of doom that hung over New York City for all of 1975. The year was bookended by bombs—Fraunce's Tavern in January, LaGuardia Airport in December—both acts of terrorism claiming random civilian casualties. In October—the night of the 16th and morning of the 17th, to be precise!—the city toed the very brink of financial collapse. When I stepped off the plane from Utah with the other passengers, we were all handed pamphlets showing a hooded skull and the bold headline WELCOME TO FEAR CITY. Inside, it warned, "Until things change, stay away from New York City if you possibly can." Strangely enough, that bit of propaganda came from a consortium of police and firemen's unions.

Nevertheless, I remember feeling glad to be home.

One last image of Jack Dunne sticks with me. We had reached base camp and the hikers were cooling off with a dip in the river. It was time for me to leave. One of the leaders and I had set off up the slope away from the water when Dunne yelled, "Wait!" He ducked into his little shelter and ran out waving a stick of dynamite above his head. "I wanna show you how we irrigate the desert, Mad Dog Dunne style!" He lit the fuse and threw the dynamite in a high, slow arc out into the middle of the river. The rolling surface swallowed it, then with a sudden deep thump, erupted in a geyser that shot water fifty feet into the air. Like a tiny storm, it drenched everyone standing on the banks, even sprinkling us on the hillside trail. Dunne cut a bizarre figure, crowing like a kid and leaping about, dressed in nothing but a blue Speedo, pleased beyond measure at his own antics.

Years and years of living can seriously erode the images of memory, but as the movie of my past played out in my mind while I drove down Route 17 in New Jersey, I felt that something was unmistakably linked between the man who called himself Lester Spanda and the man who called himself Jack Dunne. Could they be brothers? Were they the same man? It seemed utterly unlikely. Yet Spanda appeared to be the right age, nearing sixty, his thinning red-blonde crewcut sprinkled with gray, his thick body just a bit softer, his unremarkable features a little more wrinkled but spiked by the same cocky grin. The caretaker of an old church in Ponckhockie was without a doubt an older, more weathered version of the man I had last seen twenty years before, mostly naked, wet, waving and whooping, deep in the Utah desert.

8: HOME

Now I had *two* reasons to go back upstate as soon as possible: one, to see the O'Briens and continue with my research, and the other to learn more about Lester Spanda.

When I got home, Cate and Ava were there, and when I asked where they'd been, Cate told me they'd tried the park, but then fled to the air-conditioning of the Newport Mall, a two-block walk from our Hamilton Park neighborhood. They sometimes hang out in the food court, where there's a little carousel for children.

"So you stayed there all afternoon?" I asked.

Cate said, "Yeah, pretty much," as she chopped vegetables, her back to me. I saw Ava glance at her, then return to the jigsaw puzzle she was putting together, without a word. And it was interesting that Cate did not ask why I had been late. That meant she was lying. The subtle cues that pass between husband and wife can say so much—so much that is unverifiable but nevertheless absolutely certain. I would just have to keep my eyes open.

Of course, I didn't volunteer the information that I had bought her a bouquet of wildflowers but had absent-mindedly left them in an oven-like car to become a sad mass of wilted weeds.

As it turned out, the following day, a Sunday, was the last full day we spent together as an unbroken family. I'm glad we had that day. If I could have predicted the future, I would have made sure we did something special. Instead, it was an entirely average Sunday, made a bit claustrophobic by the ongoing heat wave. I tried to sleep late while Cate was up extra early and out for a run, her unbreakable routine altered to accommodate the weather. Ava bounced on my bed for a while as I attempted to fool her with exaggerated snoring noises, then she went to the living room to play her My Little Pony video for the hundredth time. I gave up on sleep and threw together a hearty scrambled-egg-and-veggie breakfast, perfectly timed for Cate's return.

We each did our own thing: newspapers, magazines, Barbie dolls, video. To an outsider it would have looked perfectly normal, but the invisible atmosphere was thick with something unspoken. Moments of no eye contact, a second-long pause in a conversation, the slightest stiffness at the corners of her mouth. These are the cues that make me assume she's angry and not telling me. But today I didn't ask; sometimes it's just too exhausting. Easier to let time do its magic. Our smiles were cordial and we maneuvered around one another, until finally I suggested we walk to the mall, and Ava leaped up with a "Yay!" Cate declined, said she hadn't been sleeping well and wanted to take a nap, so Ava and I would get a couple of hours together: play for her, relief for me. All these years later, I'm grateful.

"Daddy, Daddy, take the camera! Let's make a movie about me, me, me!" She jumped on every word like a pogo stick. I grabbed the HandyCam and we walked to the mall. Cate and I often joked about Ava being a born director. If there was a camera nearby, she became the boss. Often she would pose us together, insisting on tiny adjustments of head and hand positions before clicking the shutter. I followed her orders and took shots of her posing flamboyantly in front of store window mannequins, dancing to the Muzak on the stair landing, and doing loud fake laughter while tossing her hair, going around and around on the kiddie carousel.

"Now interview me, Daddy!" She sat on a bench, I

pointed the camera and pushed Record, and before I could even ask a question, she said, "I want to talk about fairies." Wearing her "serious face," and with exaggerated nodding and a raised finger, she launched into an educational lecture. "Fairies are our friends, but we can't see them. Mostly we can't. Only I can see them. And they whisper whisper whisper..."—her voice dropped to a whisper as she cupped her ear—"...in our ears, at night. They help us, like, to, um, to say the right words, and to dance good." She kept going without prompting, ten minutes worth, and then said, "Okay, cut. That's all." And she hopped down from the bench.

Back at home, the evening was more relaxed than the morning had been. As always, Cate and I discussed our plans for the coming week. It would be a busy one for her as she continued working on a couple of freelance design projects I knew she had underway. My plan was to do more research on my Revolution film, so Ava would be going to her usual daycare center at a neighbor's house most of the week.

In bed, Cate and I gave each other a goodnight peck, then didn't touch, sinking from silence into sleep. In retrospect, I wish we had made love one last time.

At 3:42 a.m., I found myself lying wide awake. Those memories of my days in the Utah desert wouldn't let me go. I climbed out of bed as gingerly as possible and tiptoed to a closet where we kept a few boxes of old keepsakes. There was a shoebox there that held stuff from my college years, and I carried it to the living room sofa. I found an envelope containing a letter that Amy Bennett had sent me from Utah a few days after she got back from the survival trip; in it she said what a lovely day it was and wondered why I had not been very nice to her on the phone. It included a handful of faded photos of herself clowning with some of the kids in the desert. I looked carefully, but Jack Dunne was not in any of the images.

I put the letter and photos back in the envelope and

turned it over to glance at its face. My breath stopped and my heart flopped. I almost dropped the envelope as if it were on fire. I could make no sense of what I was seeing. The return address, handwritten in 1975, said: Amy Bennett, 1777 Kingston Circle, Provo, UT.

1777 Kingston Circle. Kingston. 1777.

I had entirely forgotten her home address, which was not remarkable as an address anyway. But here I was finding it again now, today, in the middle of this project, when suddenly, that word and those numerals take on an entirely new power. Why? This was a coincidence beyond what my mind could grasp. Yet what choice is there: the mind must accept what the eyes feed it.

I sat there for a long time. I could not figure out any way that this fit into what I was doing, into my research or my film. It had no meaning. It just was.

Finally I put the envelope and its contents back into the shoebox, which went back into the closet. My eyelids were heavy and I crawled back into bed and slept.

I had a dream. On waking I thought nothing of it, but later it seemed to grow in significance. The plot details are missing, but the essential images were of a house on a cul-de-sac—my house, number 1777, where I lived with either Amy or Cate, I wasn't sure. The house was built of wood but the wood was rotten, full of termites like maggots in dead flesh. It stank. Then the house caught fire, and burned completely to the ground in a giant conflagration. I thought I should grieve, but when I saw that what remained was a perfect stone foundation on which a new house could be built, I was happy.

That morning, Monday, I felt haunted by a sense of mysterious forces just outside my conscious awareness. Even coffee couldn't shake it, but I said nothing to Cate and we went about our planned day.

I called the O'Briens again. A stranger's voice, a man's,

answered with a flat tone, "O'Brien residence." When I asked to speak with Randall, the man said "May I ask what this is regarding?" I wondered, with a faint sense of alarm, why they would be screening calls in this formal way, but I explained briefly that I had missed my appointment yesterday and was hoping to reschedule for an interview regarding my film in development.

The man was silent for a moment. Then he said, "I'm very sorry, Mr. Rose, but there's been a tragedy. The O'Briens will not be meeting with you. I'm not at liberty to say anything more at this time. Please accept my apology." He hung up.

Stunned, I debated calling back immediately. But if what he said was true, then I would just be an intrusive stranger. I didn't want that, so I set my hopes on a positive change in the future and I let it go.

Next, I called Nils Nilsson. He was friendly and invited me to visit him at the Schuylerville library and he'd give me some insider information about the Saratoga battlefield. We made a plan for the coming Thursday.

9: HISTORY

Those were the days when researching anything in the world by sitting in one place and clicking a mouse was not yet even imagined by most earth-dwellers. I had a passing awareness that there were websites for "searching" but I still preferred libraries, books, physical contact. Monday I spent at the Jersey City Public Library, Tuesday at the New York City Public Library, scribbling notes, making copies, jotting ideas for new story angles and for the structure of an entire series of films about the Revolution—a "people's history" series.

My thoughts returned frequently to the address on the envelope, but then I would shove the image away and continue with the labor at hand: finding facts, uncovering stories.

I was like a terrier after a rat; single-minded, unstoppable. Surely, it was unbalanced—but at the time, I didn't know that. Obscure facts with strange relationships, coincidences, contradictions, enigmas... I dug and dug and forgot everything else. What was I doing? Following my father's footsteps? Escaping mundane present reality? Enacting my destiny? Maybe all those and more.

I liked the parallel: Kingston's temporary status as the New York capital, similar to New York City's temporary status as the US capital.

I loved finding tidbits like this: The Green-Wood Cemetery in Brooklyn is the site of the first big battle of the Revolutionary War, in which the American colonists were severely defeated and fled across the East River to upper Manhattan. Buried there is a man named—no relationship to the cemetery name, ha!—John Greenwood. He was a 16-year-old who walked from Maine to Boston to join the Continental Army, playing his fife all the way. Later he became the dentist who made George Washington's teeth.

And this: Washington was once in love with a woman named Mary, who rejected him to marry his friend and rival, of the wealthy Morris family. As the revolution began, Morris was a loyalist and fled with Mary, his wife. Out of all possible sites, it was their mansion that General Washington commandeered to be his headquarters. Later, as President, he hosted his entire cabinet for dinner there. The Morris Mansion still stands as the oldest house in Manhattan.

I felt driven by some obsessive force to ferret out these quirky factoids that personalize history, not only as background for my story on the burning of Kingston, but as potential new lines of inquiry, new films. If a story contained some kind of reversal, paradox, mirror image, I pursued it like a fish after a worm. I was hooked. But that evening, if my enthusiasms threatened to bubble over at dinner, I kept them contained. Cate and I had a delicate balance. She thought I was wasting time, so to avoid conflict, we stuck to banal small talk.

I resisted my urge to blurt about the great fire that consumed up to twenty-five percent of Manhattan in September of 1776, just 13 months before the Kingston burning. The British had just taken over the city and reports came in from both sides, conflicting accounts of either rebels or loyalists witnessed starting the fires. Blame ricocheted, but no conclusions were reached. Both sides were guilty! I imagined the residents, people who just wanted to go on with their lives but were denied by the forces of politics. The destruction was terrible.

On Wednesday I braved the brutal heat and made my

way downtown by subway and foot, to the oldest part of Manhattan. I felt my skin ooze in the grimy tunnels, and I revisited my memories of the desert, that other kind of heat, in which one bakes instead of boiling. I walked from site to site:

Bowling Green, where Americans tore down the gold-coated statue of King George III, broke it to pieces, and melted his lead body for bullets to fire at his soldiers.

City Hall Park and Golden Hill, where, on two occasions years before the war started, American blood was shed by British soldiers with bayonets.

City Hall Park, where Washington read the new Declaration of Independence to his troops... where citizens fleeing the great fire huddled for safety... where later the worst British prisons stood and hundreds of American POWs died. Where today stands a statue of martyred patriot spy Nathan Hale, although three other sites in the city claim to be where he was hanged.

Trinity Church, whose original edifice was burned to ruins in the fire, then turned by the British into a pleasure garden hung with paper lanterns.

Federal Hall, site of the first American Congress in 1765, which then became British headquarters during the war, then later where the new US Federal Government was established in 1789 and George Washington was inaugurated. Where the Bill of Rights was introduced.

My commie father walked every one of these streets, and so many more. I don't know if he was aware of the history buried under the pavement. Did he see the same ghosts I did?

Finally, I relaxed with a cheeseburger and a cold beer at old Fraunces Tavern on Pearl Street, remodeled after its 1975 bombing. The building originally built as a mansion for Stephen DeLancey, loyalist leader, but later where the Sons of Liberty met in secret to plan their audacious revolution. Where a British cannonball crashed through the roof in 1775, where an American victory banquet was held as the British evacuated the city, and where George Washington said farewell to his officers at the war's end. A building destroyed by fire more than once in the 1800s, so that today we know nothing of its original structure and appearance.

Everywhere I turned, there was fire.

10: BATTLEFIELD

On Thursday I got an early start and drove up the Thruway again, the day hot but not as hot as Saturday had been. I kept the windows down, let the breeze blow into the sleeves of my loose shirt, did my best to stay cool. I sped north, up the Thruway to Albany and then up the "Northway" as they call it, parallel with the Hudson, until I saw the exit that would take me to Schuylerville. Nilsson had given some basic driving directions and I easily found the Schuylerville Public Library, parked on the street, and went in.

When I asked the lady at the desk for Nils Nilsson, she said, "Who?" I repeated myself and she said, "I'm sorry, I don't know who that is. Did you think he was an employee here?"

I fished in my pocket and pulled out the business card he had given me, and showed it to her. I said, "I spoke to him just a couple days ago and made an appointment to meet him here today."

She looked at the card and said, "I'm sorry, I don't know what's going on, but this is not even one of our business cards." She picked up a card from a holder on the desk. "See, take a look at this one. The color and the logo are different. And *I'm* the library director, not this Nilsson guy. He gave you a completely fake card."

I was speechless; my mouth must have been hanging open. "Wow," I said. "Just...wow. I don't know why he would do that. Was he...? I wonder if I'm being scammed in some way."

She just stared at me. "Is there a phone I can use?" I said.

She directed me to a pay phone in the entryway and I called the number on the card Nilsson had given me, the same number at which I'd spoken to him on Monday. A recording: *this number is no longer in service.* I turned the card over and dialed the number scrawled in pencil on the back—his home, he had said. I got the same recording. What was going on?

Lies, all lies.

Next I called Cate at the office. She answered, told me she was working on her freelance project, everything was fine, and asked why I called. There was an odd formality in her tone.

"Well…I don't really know," I said. "The guy I was supposed to meet stood me up and I can't reach him. He didn't call there, did he?"

"Nope, no calls," she said.

"Hmm…well, okay, I'm going to spend a couple more hours here looking at the Saratoga battlefield, then I'm coming home. See you, oh, late this afternoon."

"Okay, bye," she said. Click. It seemed that I had interrupted her concentration, that she just wanted to get back to her work. Okay, fine.

I picked up a leaflet from the library that showed the directions to the battlefield park and the monuments. I drove first to the closest spot, the monument where British General Burgoyne had surrendered to American General Gates on October 17, 1777—the most important day of the war for the Americans, the turning point that led to victory. A hundred miles to the south, Kingston was a smoldering ruin after its citizens had desperately fought the fires set the previous day by a different army of redcoats.

The monument was like a great stone spike in the summer sky. On the four sides of its base, above head height, were arched niches. In three of those niches were impressive bronze statues in noble military poses: Generals Gates and Schuyler, Colonel Morgan. The pamphlet said the fourth was the space for General Benedict Arnold. It was empty.

I knew there was no actual connection between me and my traitorous namesake, but my spirit suddenly sank. Was this the monument Nils Nilsson had referred to—Nils Nilsson, the liar? Was this some sort of cruel joke? But he couldn't have known my full name or history.

I dutifully shot a few photos, then looked inside the monument, considering climbing the staircase to the top for the wide views of the landscape. But the walls held huge bronze plaques, melodramatic scenes in bas-relief that were clearly just patriotic propaganda. I was in no mood for that. I turned my back on the monument and drove a few miles south to the battlefield site.

At the Visitor's Center I picked up a stack of materials and a guide brochure, then drove directly to the spot that said "Arnold" on the map, a site known as the Breymann Redoubt during the battle. Inside an iron fence stood a granite tablet like a gravestone. It was the backdrop for a lifelike carving of a tall military boot hanging on a post. The other side of the tablet held a carved inscription that included these words: "In memory of the most brilliant soldier of the Continental Army, who was desperately wounded on this spot, winning for his countrymen the decisive battle of the American Revolution, and for himself the rank of Major General."

The heroic officer was not named.

But in the guide brochure, I read this: "Arnold led one column in a series of savage attacks on the Balcarres Redoubt, a powerful British fort built on Freeman's Farm. Failing repeatedly to carry this position, Arnold wheeled his horse and, dashing through both armies' crossfire, spurred northwest to the Breymann Redoubt. Arriving as American troops began to assault the fortification, he joined the final surge overwhelming the German soldiers defending it. Entering the redoubt he was wounded in the leg. Had he died there, posterity would have known few brighter names than Benedict Arnold."

I sat in the shade on a bench and perused more of the printed material I'd picked up. I learned about Arnold's brave and intelligent leadership in actions like the capture of Fort Ticonderoga, defensive and delaying tactics in the Battle of Valcour Island on Lake Champlain and the Battle of Ridgefield, Connecticut, operations in relief of the Siege of Fort Stanwix, and more. He had been well-respected but not always well-liked; he made enemies easily, and his ideas were often opposed. Even his heroics at Saratoga were in defiance of General Gates, with whom he'd had a shouting match the day before. More than once he was passed over for advancements he felt he deserved, and made protests to Congress and the Army about politically-motivated promotions. Wounded several times, his left leg now two inches shorter than his right, he wrote of his feelings in a letter to George Washington: "Having become a cripple in the service of my country, I little expected to meet [such] ungrateful returns." Along with resentment grew his pessimism about America's future. But during the same years, he was given honors and advancements: command of Montreal, of Philadelphia, of West Point, and he exploited every position for both prestige and money.

My father was only partially right: yes, Arnold was mistreated by the power structure, as were many others. But he was also ambitious and power-hungry, not one of the common men at all. He was complicated and passionate, an intelligent visionary with a driving self-interest, a survivor. He turned his treason into a generalship in the British Army, a large cash payment, and a comfortable future with a large family. He died in London at the age of sixty.

And now I saw the predicament of monument-makers:

how do you honor a man who was a genuine hero one moment, but a traitor the next? The Victory Monument and the Boot Monument were their solution.

All this felt strangely disorienting, a rug pulled out from under my feet. All these years I'd been wearing a story about my namesake as if it were my own, and it had always been a shallow mistake. The real man was not merely a cartoon coward, a cardboard traitor as taught in textbooks, but something much more nuanced, even a brave hero. This name that I carried, that had caused me so much pain, this ghost following me around, this burden on my shoulders... I was glad to be able to let it go. I felt a weight lifted, I felt a relief to know something that perhaps should have been obvious, but only now could I accept it. This: every person has multiple selves. Every person plays different roles on the stage of his life, at different times, according to different circumstances. I do the same, everyone does, so I should not judge. I should always want to know more. About the other or about myself.

My father had thought he was doing a good thing when he gave me my burdensome name. He also had been my hero one day, my nemesis the next, like every son's father. I made this silent vow: on the monument to my father inside my chest, I will not make him invisible.

I had no handkerchief so I lifted up my shirt to mop my sweaty forehead and continued my tour of the battlefield. As I drove, walked, drove and walked through the fields, where blue posts marked American positions and red marked British, I stared at the vistas and read about how the battle had unfolded across that landscape. I imagined the noise, the smoke, the blood on the ground, the bodies. I felt solemn. I did not feel any sort of patriotic inspiration, but it did seem that this was war that had a just cause. Surely had I been living then, I would have felt so. War had changed. In modern times there had not been a war that felt "just" since WWII. Certainly our murderous blasting of the Iraqis in Kuwait a few years earlier was nothing but disgusting and shameful.

Those were the thoughts I remember having at the time, in 1995. I obviously had no idea how much worse it would get over the next twenty years.

After a couple of hours at the battlefield, I felt I understood enough. I'd taken numerous notes and snapshots and spied a few angles where I would want to come back with a film crew and shoot some coverage. I decided it was time to head south again. I didn't know what to do about the Nils Nilsson mystery. I was glad he had directed me to the battlefield, but beyond that, I just had to shrug it all off as a freak occurrence in which I had met a genuine nutcase.

11: CHANCE

Because of Nilsson's no-show I was ahead of schedule, so I decided to stop off in Kingston and visit Lester Spanda, talk to him a bit, decide whether or not I would ask him about the past. I pulled off at exit 19, cruised through Kingston, down to the Rondout, and into the sleepy little Ponckhockie neighborhood. On a whim, I turned up the O'Briens' street first. There was a van at their house with its rear doors open, and two workmen were exiting the open front door, followed by another man with a clipboard. At the risk of being overly pushy, I stopped, got out, and approached him.

"Hello," I said. "Are the O'Briens moving? I'm a friend."

"You haven't heard the news then," he said to me, frowning. I recognized the voice I had heard on the phone on Monday. The man was tall with an angular face and dark hair, a forties movie-star look.

"I called on Monday about trying to reset an appointment. I was just passing by today—."

He interrupted me, asked my name, and I told him, repeating the facts about my film as the men in the van drove away. His serious expression deepened as he moved closer and looked me in the eyes.

"Mr. Rose, the O'Brien family were in accident on the Thruway on Saturday. There was a terrible car fire and... and the only survivor was little Ethan, who is still in Kingston hospital."

I was too stunned to speak. He went on, "The funeral services for Randall, Bridget, and Emily were held yesterday at a church nearby. I'm sorry you were not notified, but it was a very small list...."

I must have looked ill, because he said, "Would you like to come in, get a drink of water? I'm a friend of the family; name is Auster. Paul." He held out a hand and I shook it, still speechless.

"Yes," I managed to say, "I need to sit."

Inside, the house was dark and cool. Almost every surface was covered with floral arrangements and the air was thick with their perfume. I moved some flowers from a sofa to the floor and sat down. Auster filled a glass from the kitchen, brought it to me, and relaxed on a wingback chair.

"Actually, I didn't know the family," I confessed. "I had talked to Randall on the phone, that's all." My voice was almost a whisper, my throat full of something. A sip of water helped a little.

He didn't respond and we sat in silence for a moment, each staring at the floor.

"It's so strange," I said. "I was right there, stuck in the traffic jam on the Thruway on Saturday. I saw the burned van. I was on my way to meet with them, here, but I was late. I was late because of their...."

Auster nodded. "There's no explaining the weirdness of chance, is there?"

"I'm having a weird week. Full of... I don't know... odd twists. I wonder what it means."

"Probably nothing, but it's damned fascinating anyway," he said with a kind smile. His presence was reassuring, his interest genuine as far as I could tell, so I just kept talking: the repeated theme of fire, the improbable Jack Dunne/Lester Spanda connection, the address on the envelope, my dream, Nilsson and the fake business card, my new insights about my traitorous namesake. Auster lit a slim little cigar and smoked as he listened. When I heard myself mentioning my fears about Cate's truthfulness, I realized it was time to shut up.

"Sorry, I didn't mean to spill like that," I said, rolling my eyes to cover the fact that I still felt spooked about it all.

Auster chuckled. "No problem, I get it. I was especially interested in what you said about the guy at the Union Congregational Church. That's where we had the funeral yesterday, and where all these flowers just came from." He looked around. "Not sure what to do with them."

I had already been planning to visit Lester Spanda. Now I had another point of connection with him besides my old memories. The strangeness kept stacking up, and I suddenly felt a shiver of premonition run through my body. Spanda, Nilsson... now Auster. Was he on the level?

"Is there any chance I could use the phone here?" I asked. "I can charge the call to my card."

"Sure, right over there. I'll meet you outside," Auster said.

I dialed our office number for the second time that day. My ripple of fear had taken me right back to thinking about that Nilsson guy. What if he had conned me into being away from home so he could burglarize our apartment, or who knows what? The office was safe, an industrial building behind locked gates at both street and elevator. But our apartment, two floors of a brownstone: not so much. I wanted to be cautious but not irrational, and I didn't want to burden Cate with my concerns. She would just be scared or angry or both.

"Hey Cate, me again. I had an idea: how about if you pick up Ava from the sitter's and you guys meet me for dinner at Luigi's, say 5:30." I didn't want them getting home to an empty apartment without me, in case that creep was there.

"Really, why?"

"Oh, I don't know, I just feel like it. I'll buy." The whole thing didn't make sense, and there was nothing in our apartment worth going to all this trouble for. But I still couldn't take any chances.

"Okay, it's a plan," she said. "See you there." We both hung up.

Outside, the afternoon heat was oppressive. "You mentioned the church," I said to Auster. "I'm heading over there right now to talk to the caretaker again. Wanna come along?"

"No, I have to get going now, but if you still need somebody upstate to assist with your research, give me a call." He handed me a business card that read Writer/Editor, with an address in Catskill. "I work for several local newspapers, so I have a lot of contacts and know this area quite well: Ulster County, Greene, Columbia, Northern Dutchess."

"Great, I appreciate this. In fact, I'll call you tomorrow and make a plan," I said as we walked toward our cars at the curb. I gave him my card as well, and we parted. On one level, I felt that I had made a new friend, but on another, I had to be wary. I tried to hold both those feelings, an ember and an ice cube, at the same time.

12: CHURCH

Over on Abruyn Street, I parked across the street from the church and walked in through the double front doors and down the central aisle of the chapel. As churches go, it was not big, and the interior seemed even smaller than I expected. The light was dim, the air distinctly cooler. There was a slightly musty smell, the odor of age.

The church seemed empty but then I heard a voice echo: "Welcome! How are you today?"

I stopped and looked around; I didn't know where the sound was coming from. Then he emerged from behind a screen near the front of the chapel, walking toward me, grinning.

"Hello hello hello! I'm the caretaker of the church, Lester Spanda." He reached out his hand to shake mine. Just as before, there was a twinkle in his eye as if he were enjoying a private joke. "Please, call me Les. Haha!"

"Hi," I said, "I was here a few days ago, and decided to come back and take you up on your offer of a tour." I had decided to play it cool, not mention the O'Briens, just scope him out.

"Yes, I remember you. So glad you returned! Well sir, let's start right here, shall we?" He opened both arms and looked toward the ceiling as if to indicate the whole world. "The Ponckhockie Union Congregational Church is the oldest reinforced concrete structure in the state of New York. That means it was at the forefront of a revolution in construction techniques that changed the look of cities all over the world. In fact, right here in the Rondout, the Newark Lime and Cement Company had a thriving business, and in 1870 they built this church as a Sunday School for the workers' families. Not exactly the way business operates today, eh?"

I was not really paying much attention; I was focused on him, comparing this man in front of me to my memories, dim though they were.

"The church is built of poured concrete made from locally mined natural cement and crushed bluestone aggregate. The structure incorporates iron reinforcing rods and plates in its buttresses, and an ingenious cold-air conditioning system inside the walls."

He went on, but after a few minutes, I stopped him.

"Actually, you know, I think I get the picture…about the church…and thank you, you're a very good, uh, tour guide," I said.

For a moment he looked disappointed to be interrupted. "Thank you. And—"

"I want to ask you about something," I said. "I have a very strong impression that you and I have met before."

"Really?" he said, "Here at the church?"

"No," I said, "Way back in the seventies in the desert in Utah."

I was almost certain I saw a shade flicker across his face, but he covered it very well, with a chuckle and a shake of the head. "Oh, I don't think so. I'm from England. Been here in Kingston for over ten years, working here in the church. I've actually never been out west."

I really was not a hundred percent positive; how could I be? I said, "Well, I guess I could be mistaken, but you have a very strong resemblance to a man I knew as Jack Dunne."

"You know, sir, I think the world is full of mysteries. Perhaps we all have a doppelganger somewhere. But my name is actually Lester Spanda." He kept moving and I followed.

Why was he so cheery? "I'm Les, Les every day, haha! Closer and closer to zero!"

Now he's making no sense at all, I thought. Maybe he's nervous. Maybe he's lying. Or, more likely, my imagination is on overdrive.

He said, "Shall we continue our tour?"

I thought: what can it hurt? So I said yes and he made a polite after-you gesture as he said, "Over here behind the altar... let me show you a truly unique feature of the construction of this building."

I moved in front of him, took a few steps, and felt a gentle touch at the base of my neck. Then nothingness.

MEANTIME

13: HUGH

Each of us walks through life as if through a tunnel. I'm in my tunnel, you're in yours. When my wife leaves for work in the morning, I have no idea what is happening to her until her tunnel intersects mine again at the end of the day. Apparently there are people with clairvoyant skills who can see into other people's tunnels, but that's not a talent I have. I've always wished I could know what someone else is experiencing at any given moment, to compare it with my own stream of experiences, like cross-cutting between parallel storylines in a movie. To be less separate... less alone, you might say. Maybe I didn't get enough cuddling as a baby.

Back in 1995, not long after I had returned to the world, I was able to find out what had been going on in the lives of those closest to me while I was having my strange adventure. But it was actually years before I heard from my old friend Hugh MacCahane about what happened to him that summer.

We had been buddies at Dickinson High School in Jersey City, "the mausoleum on the mount," in the days when no one ever called him anything but HueyMac, one word. He and Arturo (Artie) Cruz and I were inseparable for those few short years, a little urban-hippie-poet tribe with art-rebel attitude. But then Hugh's parents moved to the suburbs in the spring of '73, our senior year, ostensibly as part of that decade's general middle-class flight from the crumbling ruin of Jersey City. More likely it was because Hugh's dad needed to distance himself from his disgraced former buddy, Mayor Thomas Whelan, ousted for corruption and headed for prison. In any case, HueyMac and I began to drift apart.

In 1974, when I was at NYU and Hugh was at Boston University, Artie died of a heroin overdose behind a dumpster in an alley off Newark Avenue. Hugh and I saw each other at the funeral, got drunk and cried together afterwards, and went our separate ways. We had not been in touch since.

During the intervening decades, I heard that he was practicing law in San Francisco and had married. I'd known his dad, so I wasn't surprised he'd left art school. Beyond that, I knew nothing. But our sisters had traded occasional cards and then more frequent emails over the years, and even shared a late-nineties Caribbean vacation. That's how HueyMac eventually learned what had happened to me.

In early 2000, I received the following letter, written in longhand on several pages of fine stationery. I've excised the irrelevant chat.

Dear Ben,

My old friend, I miss you. Sentimental just now, even booze-free (4 yrs sober, AA and all, another story). Remembering our youthful escapades, mon Dieu! *...*

If Bridget's story of Emma's story of your story is true, you and I need to talk, brother. I presume nothing about your experience, but here are the facts about mine:

On July 20, 1995, I went blind. It was a Thursday afternoon and I was at a bar, into my second martini. That morning a judge had rejected my filings on a bullshit corporate litigation I was handling. I was boiling with rage, but not just at the judge. More at myself for the monumental cliché my life had become: pressured by Big Daddy into law school, following the prescribed path all the way, house in the suburbs, two kids, wife who's fucking her boss. Jesus Hieronymus Christ, I was even pretending to still be a Catholic, Oy!

So I was nursing my drink, all wrapped in self-pity, and I thought about you. With envy. I didn't really know, but I assumed you had stayed true to your dreams, out there making movies somewhere, happy as a pig in shit. All this just a way to make myself feel even worse, of course. I wanted what you had.

That's when a murky darkness started gathering around the edges of my vision. It narrowed down to a little hole through which I could just see the olive in my glass, then it winked out to black.

Once I realized I hadn't just drunkenly closed my eyes, I nearly lost my cool right there in public. The bartender called 911, I went to the hospital, had tests up the wazoo, no answers, etc etc. "Hysterical blindness"—haha, turns out it actually exists. "Conversion disorder" is its real name, a psychiatric problem, of course. Hired a home health aid so the wife wouldn't be inconvenienced, spent time with my scared kids, dutifully went to a shrink, etc etc.

But primarily I sat in my little office/den, my man-cave, and thought about things. My life. The things I hadn't done. Not big things. Just the little ways I had spent my hours, and how I intended to spend the hours that remained.

On August 3rd, my sight returned. Again, it was afternoon. I was sitting in my recliner imagining a lovely borderline between curved forms, one a smooth burgundy, the other a textured cool gray. Then, without any sort of warning, I found myself blinking, aware of an alternating lightness and darkness. The room came into focus, dim in the late sunlight filtered through curtains. No lights on, but I had to squint anyway.

My eyes have been perfectly normal ever since. Despite my shrink's fancy talk, I knew there was no valid explanation in his diagnostic codebook. I didn't care to explain it, I only cared to follow what I'd learned. It wasn't really so hard to get mental health disability pay, then a severance package, to handle my own divorce case and get shared custody, to live much more simply in a little apartment with a part time job at an art supply store. Nothing was very hard, as long as I could paint. So that's what I've been doing.

Then I learned about your experience. Granted, third hand.

But precisely the same dates! Is it fucking true? If so, no words are possible. Coincidentally incomprehensible.

Yet not.

I love you, brother. Write or call, we must *get together. ...*

Vive la résistance!

Looking joyfully forward,

HueyMac

14: CATE

After I had returned to the world but before Cate and I had resumed communication, I was able to get my old video-editing computer back—the one that had been in our office on Communipaw Avenue before everything changed—and I found an audio recording on the hard drive. It caught my attention because it was not in a project folder; it was just hanging out there among the program icons on the desktop, and it was named "To_Ben.wav." I double-clicked it and immediately heard Cate's voice. I had always loved her voice, its rich smoothness. This time it was a near-whisper, close to the mike, breathy, sad.

"Ben, where are you? Are you alive? Are you hurt? You can't do this. You can't just disappear. You can't be gone from home for two weeks without a word."

There was a pause, then her tone changed.

"What the fuck is going on, Ben? If you've abandoned Ava, I swear I'll track you down and it won't be pretty. Me, okay, so it goes, we fell apart somewhere along the way. But Ava's a baby; she needs you!"

Another pause, longer this time, then a deep breath. I quickly plugged in headphones so I could hear her deep, sexy voice right inside my ear, close enough to be my own.

"Ben, I'm going to tell you the truth. You may never hear this, but I'm going to say it anyway.

"It started July first—Saturday, but of course you were working. I was with Ava in the mall food court; you know how she loves that little carousel. I was bored, needing some adult conversation to break up the endless kid stuff, you know. Or maybe you don't know. Anyway, there was a guy sitting there, eating a Nathan's hot dog with sauerkraut. I said hello, he said hello, we chatted for a while. Just small talk, shopping, weather, nothing.

"A week later, Saturday again, same place, Ava's on the carousel. The guy's there again. This time he's reading one of my favorite obscure old books, *Thoughts on Design* by Paul Rand. I asked him why he was reading that book of all books. 'Well,' he says, 'I'm trying to design a logo and business card for myself and I don't know what I'm doing.'

"I'm trying to give you a picture now. I have to, to relive it, I don't know why. He's a tallish guy, slender, sort of average looking, but dressed in really nice clothes—silk, linen, tailored, muted colors, hip but restrained, classy. Brown hair combed straight back, graceful hands, a confident air. Seems like a successful man, a man with money. Definitely not the usual mall-walker from the neighborhood."

I was beginning to get uneasy. Where was this leading?

"I tell him I'm a designer, maybe I can help him. No hesitation— 'You're on,' he says. I ask, 'What's your business?' 'PI,' he says. I guess I looked blank, so he says, 'Private Investigator—you know, Sam Spade, Philip Marlowe.' He's smiling so I'm not sure he's serious.

"I say, 'Really? People still do that work? And make a living?' He says, 'Sure, but actually it's nothing like the old detective stories, it's much more boring, mostly computer database searches, public records, stuff like that. An occasional dull surveillance, sitting for hours while nothing happens.'

"He said he was a former cop who wanted more independence, less bureaucracy, so he started his own agency. An agency of one. I asked what he was doing in the food court of the mall, was he on a job? Tracking a sinister shopping fiend? No, he said, it was just a place he likes to come to do his reading, something about the bustle, the presence of people, because sometimes his business is lonely. He took one of my hands in his and placed a card in my palm—plain, white, no logo: *Nate Nixon, Investigation Services*. He kept holding my hand and I'm sure I was blushing. I joked, 'I doubt I'll ever need your services—my life is distinctly lacking in mystery or drama, haha!'"

I had a sour taste in my mouth. Cate paused again and the laugh in her voice disappeared.

"Shit... I'm babbling... all this doesn't matter. What matters is that I wanted him. There was a magnetic pull in my body that I hadn't felt since... since I met you. Nothing had happened, but I was guilty. So I took his design job and didn't tell you.

"And... it wasn't the first time I had lied by omission. I had done two other jobs for new clients during the spring that I never told you about. Put the money away in an account for myself. Something in me, for a long time, has been needing separation, autonomy."

She paused and sniffled; her voice trembled with choked-back tears. My face had been gradually growing hot as I listened.

"I'm confessing, Ben. I'm not proud, but I'm also not sorry. There's no going back. On that super-hot Saturday that you went upstate, I lied about what Ava and I were doing. Yes, we went to the mall for a short time. I met Nate there and told him some of my ideas for his logo and his whole business identity: card, stationery, brochure. He loved my ideas, so I felt happy and excited to get started. I took Ava to the office and let her fingerpaint while I started working on designs for Nate."

So that's why there was no answer when I called her that day. I took a deep breath, then another. Nothing was a surprise anymore, but that doesn't stop the feelings. I couldn't seem to get enough air. Cate kept talking.

"I... I couldn't help myself. I fell in love with him. That next week while you were in the city and Ava was at the sitter's, he came to the office to look at some design drafts, choose from a few options. The chemistry between us was so strong... you remember, like you and I had? We focused on business but every minute we were swimming in an erotic ocean. He kissed me when he left, and I kissed him back."

I clicked the Pause button. Hurt, angry, yes—but also stunned. Why would she tell me this, in this way? There was no tremor in her voice now, it was low and strong and sexy. But this level of detail was nothing but cruel. Was she really this nasty, vindictive, goddamned brutal? I hit Play.

"Then on that Thursday when you went up to Saratoga, he came to the office again to see the final work. Ben, we made love on the sofa in the office. More than once. Your first call was almost an interruption, but I handled it. I lied outright, and it was worth it. My god, the way he made me feel! Even now, I want him inside me. You can't know... this is *my* feeling, mine!"

My eyes were closed, and a black gulf was threatening to swallow me. Suddenly she filled my ears with a piercing, wordless wail that started low and grew higher and louder until I had to wrench the headphones off.

"Fuck! Fuck fuck fuck! Ben, what are you doing, you asshole, you shithead! Where are you?"

For a full minute she moaned and sobbed. Then she gradually calmed, and through sniffles, she picked up right where she'd left off.

"Nate had just left the office when you called to suggest we meet for dinner. So what happened? Why did you never show up?

"Ava and I went to Luigi's and we sat there and we waited; we even ordered some food, assuming you were running a little late. We waited, we ate, and you never came.

I was getting really angry—you know how I hate getting no communication like that. Maybe it was even easier to be mad at you, to deflect my own guilt. But something in me felt powerful, and it channeled into rage. So, we'd been there almost two hours when I gathered up Ava, paid the bill that you were supposed to pay, and left. I thought, did you forget the plan and just go home, you asshole? But you weren't there either. So that's when I started to get worried. I waited, I paced, I tried not to show Ava my fear. By this time it was dark, like 9:00, and I felt like I needed to do something. I started by calling our friends, asking if they'd heard from you. Nicky, Mitchell, Sharon. No luck. I called Dean Sundell, even though I knew you weren't at the stage of hiring a cameraman yet. I thought maybe you guys went out for a drink or something. Dean said no, he hadn't heard from you at all, had no idea. I didn't want to alarm your sister or mother down in Florida, decided to wait on that. But now it was approaching 11:00. I had to do more. I called the Jersey City police and they were extremely unhelpful. Clearly just dismissing me as a neurotic nagging wife, or the woman who doesn't want to believe her husband has left her for someone else. Patronizing pricks. They suggested I call the New York State highway police since you were traveling the Thruway, and I also could contact the police in the towns you had visited. Although I didn't really know what those were. Same attitude from these cops—tough shit, lady. No reports. A couple of accidents but you weren't in them.

"Next—the Yellow Pages. Hospitals, anywhere along your route. Way too many, but I tried a few, got nowhere. No trace of you, no trace! Finally I just gave up and went to bed, but I couldn't sleep. I was lying there staring at the ceiling when it occurred to me—I had someone to go to who would know just what to do. A private eye. Okay, so it may not seem appropriate, but right then, finding you was more important than any other complications.

"I called Nate even though it was 3 a.m.. He said he would take care of it, no need to file a missing person report with the police because that was just a bureaucratic thing that was ineffective anyway. We met the next morning at the mall and I gave him a picture of you and did my best to describe what you were wearing, your car and license plate, everything. I told him you'd gone to Saratoga, called me from upstate but I don't know where, and that's all I knew. He said to let him know immediately if you called again or showed up at home, and to not tell anybody or answer questions from strangers. Meanwhile he would get to work. To find you.

"So you may think, wait a minute, why would he want to find me? My rival would want me out of the picture, wouldn't he? But he's not like that, he's professional and honest. If he's going to win me, it will be fair and square. He said that. And he was very sweet and supportive when he saw how upset I was. But I wouldn't let him kiss me in front of Ava, don't worry."

Now she was making me feel like vomiting, this nauseating adoration, this gullibility. What had happened to Cate's sharp mind?

"The days went by. Ava was sad and worried; I had to lie and tell her you were on a business trip and would be home soon. Your mom and Emma both surprised me. They had nothing to offer but," (her voice pitched high in parody), "'be patient, he loves you, he'll come back.'

"Nate was not turning up any clues. He called me twice a day. We had some sweet daytime hours together, but he always had to get back to the investigation. I wanted him in my bed, but I didn't do that, I was good. Ha—my lover can't be with me 'cause he's gotta search for my husband, ha ha!"

She stopped talking to giggle like a lunatic.

"Oh, it's just so, so… fucked up, right? Right? So… then I got that call from a friend of yours I'd never heard of, Paul somebody. He said he was calling because he had expected to hear from you over a week earlier and he wanted to follow up. He said he'd seen you in Kingston the previous Thursday and you were headed for some church. That was way more information than I had, so I said goodbye to him and called Nate.

"Nate says, 'Okay, that's excellent intelligence, good work. I'm on my way to check it out. Sit tight, my love.' He called me 'my love.' You never called me that even once, you *fuck!*"

She shouted the last word, changed in a blink from sickly sweet to vicious. The voice in my head wanted to argue, *But wait, I said other words, just as good!* But she didn't pause.

"And now, and now, what have you done? Nate has not called me in three days. His phone just rings and rings. You've *both* disappeared! What am I supposed to do? *What am I supposed to do?*"

She took a deep breath for a long count, let it out, and her voice came back to a calm center, calm but strangely flat.

"I'm sure you're wondering why I would record this. It's very simple: I've reached my limit. Truth, that's all I want. The relief of truth. I think you've abandoned us, in the most cowardly way a man ever could. Okay. Whatever. You have to live with it. Ben, I'm going to be okay. I'm strong, I'm a mother, and Ava is my first priority. I'll focus on her. But I just want to know what's going on. That's all, I just want to know."

Then there were muffled noises, things moved around on the desk, fingers on the microphone, and her mutter off-mic, "Shit, what am I doing, this is just stu—."

The recording ended. I closed the player and noticed the date on the file: August 3rd, the day I got free of my prison.

15: PAUL

I learned later that my new friend Paul kept extensive journals; he had two entire shelves of red notebooks. After my escape, he visited me at the little cabin in the woods where I was hiding. He brought supplies but he also dropped a sheaf of papers on the table, saying, "When you're bored, read this; you might find it interesting."

"What is it?"

"My notes, or maybe I should say my obsessive scribblings. Just some thoughts about recent events."

The papers were photocopies from a spiral-bound graph-paper tablet, page after page of his small, neat handwriting on a pale grid of squares. This is what they said:

<<Saturday July 15>> *The dear O'Brien family. I have no words.*

<<Sunday July 16>> *Gratitude that little Ethan in his child seat was thrown clear of the car before the flames began. Broken ribs and a severe concussion were all he got. The emotional trauma may end up being the worst of it for him. Now the details are my job—I must transcend my black mood to put together a memorial service, to arrange for burial, to do all the things one never imagines doing for friends.*

<<Monday July 17>> *It seems there is no one but me to be responsible for Ethan's care. Randall was an only child, his father gone, no one knows where, since Randall was a baby. His mother now in a nursing home. Bridget's parents dead in a plane crash, her only sibling a brother with Down syndrome in assisted living.*

I had taken immediate action Saturday night to contact my friend who's a probate court judge. Randall and Bridget left no will of any kind, and without competent relatives, close family friends are next in line. So as of this afternoon I've been appointed administrator of their estate. Ethan will be the only heir to what little property there is. But intestate death statutes are less clear about what happens to minor children. In the final analysis, Ethan will be a ward of the state unless I can arrange something different.

<<Tuesday July 18>> I've established my credentials with Kingston Hospital; they know me there now. I took Sophie with me this evening, since Ethan has always liked her. It gave her a chance most eight-year-olds don't get, to face something big and serious, and rise to the occasion to help someone else. Siri was unable to come because of a meeting with the editor of her imminent second novel, but she'll join us there soon. Poor little Ethan cries for his mother and we can't even promise that she'll be here soon. We can't hold him because of his broken ribs. We stroke his arms and his head and tell him we know he's sad and scared but we love him and we're there to help him.

<<Wednesday July 19>> The funeral for Randall, Bridget, and Emily was held today at Ponckhockie Union Congregational Church. Attendees were mostly from the neighborhood and the church, but there were several city friends of theirs, even some folks I had known as well, from the Manhattan days before R and B moved up here. I tried to speak to everyone, not sure I succeeded.

<<Thursday July 20>> I had just finished moving all the flowers from the church to the O'Brien home when a guy drove up in a small silver hatchback, a Hyundai. Medium height, stocky build, dark hair, trimmed beard, dressed for the heat in cargo shorts, sandals, a tropical shirt. Calls himself Ben Rose. He claimed to have missed an appointment with Randall, wanted to reschedule, and didn't know about the accident. Judging by his reaction to the news, I took him at his word. He needed to sit down and collect himself, so we talked for a few minutes. Immediately, I was fascinated by the way reality folds back on itself, negates itself, or

perhaps by the way each person is in his own time stream with his own perception of cause and effect, and these time streams may intersect, but rarely with the expected results.

Fact: the planned meeting of Rose and O'Brien does not happen. Why does it not happen? Ultimately, it's because the O'Briens are dead. But to Rose, it's because he's late, delayed by an accident on the highway. He doesn't know that the accident delaying him is in fact the ultimate end, the final fiery moments, of the very people he had intended to meet. Nor does he think, until later (or not?), about the possibility that, if the O'Briens had not had an appointment with him, they may not have been on that highway on that hot afternoon, hurrying back home to meet him. They may not have met their deaths. It cannot rationally be said that he caused their deaths, but there is nevertheless an undeniable connection.

Also, a conundrum: his need was the very cause of the event that denied the fulfillment of his need. The creation of his goal canceled out the achievement of his goal—an impossibility, as in 1 $= -1$.

Rose had never met the O'Briens, yet he had a unique, even profound, relationship with them. Out of the hundreds of people delayed on the Thruway that day, delayed by the deaths of the O'Briens, he was the only one who was on his way to meet them. It's safe to say that within that set of delayed people, the O'Briens lived in no one's mind but his. It's probably also safe to say that none of those people had been in the minds of Randall and Bridget O'Brien that day, that hour—only Rose. These two parties, two cars like capsules in space, were on a collision course of some sort, a collision that was actualized only in some other, non-physical dimension. A meeting not of bodies but in the field of consciousness.

Enough of that. It's late.

<<Friday July 21>> *I scribbled until I was tired last night, but I've had many more thoughts about yesterday. I sat there in the thick perfume of flowers, listening to Rose, and I didn't show how I*

was gripped by all the synchronicities and strange twists he rattled on about.

First, he talked about fire. He's a filmmaker researching a film about the American Revolution, and he keeps encountering stories of fire.

Fraunce's Tavern, where the secret society called the Sons of Liberty met to plan the revolution... it burned several times in later years, so now no one knows what it originally looked like. Fire as a mask, a disguise. Or fire as a code that hides the original text, a cipher that cannot be deciphered. Fire as a thief, a thief of history.

In September 1776, while the British occupied New York, much of Manhattan burned in a blaze that the British claimed was set by the Americans and the Americans claimed was set by the British. Fire as visible symbol of the energy of conflict, the soul of war made manifest. Fire as blind force of nature, spontaneous combustion without human cause, an inescapable fact of physics. Fire—its intangible nature, its destructive force—as a metaphor for lies.

Also, there was his dream of a house built of rotten wood that burns to the foundation: fire as a cleansing, purifying agent.

Add to that: fire gives light, drives back darkness. Makes a safe space, a campfire in the vast primeval night. A torch lights a forest path—but only for a moment before blackness closes in. Fire grants sight, reveals what was hidden. See it now, before it's gone!

Fire, stolen from the gods by Prometheus, for humans, gaining him eternal punishment. Fire as the ultimate gift.

Then, to bring it all grimly to the immediate present... Rose's film focuses on the burning of Kingston in 1777, when the O'Brien home was the first building torched by the redcoats. And now they die in a car fire.

Fire as fate, the turning of a great invisible wheel.

These are all my thoughts alone, not Rose's words at all.

He kept talking. He told me about what may be an incredible coincidence—meeting a man a few days ago in a Kingston church whom he'd first met twenty years ago in a Utah desert—or, if not a re-meeting, then an equally strange doppelganger encounter.

My thoughts: perhaps an even more frightening possibility is that the utterly convincing similarity of two men can be manufactured in one's own mind. A memory forced into current consciousness for some reason, a lesson to be learned. But why?

And then something even more spooky. When he first met the man in 1975, he was visiting Utah with his college girlfriend. A few days ago, he found an old letter from her and discovered that her home address had been 1777 Kingston Circle. A direct reference to his life today, twenty years later. No real connection, only the invisible one in his mind, his life.

The question arises: were those letters and numbers implanted in his subconscious like a seed that grew to become the subject of his film today? Or... is time not really linear? Does the present somehow exert an influence on the past, a circular effect (Kingston Circle!) like an eddy in the ocean of a vast simultaneous Now?

He went on. Just that afternoon he had encountered inexplicable human behavior: a man he'd met in the traffic jam on the Thruway had given him a business card that was entirely a fake, leading him to a place he may never have gone otherwise. Why? The place it had led him was to the Saratoga battlefield and two monuments where Benedict Arnold was simultaneously present and absent, honored and dishonored, remembered and forgotten. A ghost of a ghost.

It was almost a case of damnatio memoriae, *that ancient Roman practice of expunging all traces of a former public figure who had fallen out of favor. But not exactly, because history remembers Arnold, so here he becomes visibly invisible, 1 = -1.*

And all this is important because Ben's name is Benedict Arnold Rose, a source of shame throughout his life. But on this visit to the battlefield, he learned that Arnold was a hero as well as a traitor. So... no person is just one thing. And more important: he felt redeemed, redeemed by a lie—the sham business card had led him there. Deceit becomes discovery.

But what else did it mean? Was it a ploy to get him away from home for some nefarious reason? No act, no event, is just one thing. *Everything in the world is operating on more than one level, always.*

I was absorbing all this and wondering why I was suddenly part of Rose's convoluted story. Clearly, I had a part to play: Siri and Sophie and I were close friends of Randall and Bridget O'Brien and their children. On a personal level, this tragedy was much more mine than his—although tragedy is never really owned by anyone. Also, I had met the man Rose was talking about—the caretaker at Ponckhockie Union Congregational Church—because we had the O'Briens' funeral there.

And speaking of the funeral... I was sitting in the congregation listening to the eulogy, holding Siri's hand, while my eyes scanned the floral arrangements. Almost obscured behind the others was a bouquet of white roses draped with a red crucifix made of ribbon. I distinctly remember musing "hmm... rose and cross... a Rosicrucian funeral." Then, the day after the funeral, yesterday afternoon, a jolt went through me when Ben Rose gave me his business card just before he drove away. It showed a logo combining a rose and a cross and said Rose/Cross Productions, Jersey City. What does this coincidence mean? I have no idea, but the simple fact of its existence is startling.

And there are other, more subtle ways I felt a connection with him. Rose told me he'd been born and raised in Jersey City. So he was a child there during the years I made so many visits with my father as he was overseeing his rental properties. Both Rose and I have the grit of Jersey City in our veins.

Also, perhaps it means something that I happen to meet a film-maker just when my head is full of thoughts about the dreamlike nature of film. Hope springs eternal... maybe my just-being-born novel—about a man's search for a long-lost movie director, and about illusions, fate, unpredictability—will fare better than all those past rejects.

I read all this and had a number of pages yet to go. I felt understood. I could see that Auster and I were on similar

wavelengths, but he was so much more thoughtful and artic-
ulate about it. I made myself a cup of coffee and settled in to
read more.

<<Saturday July 22>> *I'm disturbed by something that hap-*
pened today, and I'm wondering if it connects somehow to Rose's
tangled but strangely ordered story. I went to Kingston Hospital to
visit Ethan and check on his treatment. I always like to stop first
at the nurse's station on Ethan's floor to see who's on duty and
hear from them about his progress. Just as I arrived at the desk,
a man came out of Ethan's room. He strode past, nodded to me,
said "Thank you, Jane" to the nurse, and continued out the door.
He was my height, slim, a face devoid of distinguishing character-
istics (which perhaps was its most distinctive feature). He was not
unique in any way except for the fact that he was dressed like a
corporate executive, the cut of his suit suggesting Wall Street rather
than medicine. "See you soon, Mr. Nachtmann," the nurse called
after him.
"Doctor Nachtmann?" I asked her.
"Oh, no, he's not a doctor," she said. "He's Ethan's rich uncle.
He's going to adopt him when he's all healed up."
"I need to speak to him," I said, and took off in pursuit. Outside
the double doors of the ward, he was nowhere to be seen in the cor-
ridor. I hurried to the stairwell, hoping I could beat the elevator
down four floors. But he was not in the elevator, nor in the lobby.
I went out to the parking lot and saw no sign of him.
Something was fishy about Mr. Nachtmann. There were two
reasons I didn't believe he was Ethan's uncle: One, according to
what Randall and Bridget had told me about their families, there
was no such brother. Two, I had seen "Mr. Nachtmann" before, and
he was not wearing that fancy suit. He drove past the church as the
last of the people were leaving the funeral, his eyes straight ahead
as if it were of no interest to him. I'm exceptionally good with faces,
even one as bland as his; I know it was him. Too bad I have no
memory of the car.

I would have to search for him later. I went back up and stood by Ethan's bed for a while as he dozed peacefully.

<<Sunday July 23>> *I slept in today. For an hour I held Siri in bed as she cried. Then I got up and did my best to catch up on a couple of articles I owed to local papers, deadlines approaching.*

<<Monday July 24>> *First thing this morning I called my friend in the hospital administration, Janice Ledig, and convinced her to tell me what was going on. She did some checking and called me back. "His name is Noel Nachtmann," she told me. "He's Bridget's half-brother, from her mother's first marriage. He lives in California, has a wife and 9-year-old son, runs an investment management firm."*

"Did he show any proof?"

"His ID looked real to my staff, but we haven't gone any further than that. It will be up to the state of New York to decide what happens next."

I still didn't believe it. Our conversations about family—mine and Siri's, Randall's and Bridget's—throughout several meals and bottles of wine, had been so thorough, I just couldn't swallow that there was a half-brother somehow omitted. I decided to just stay alert and ask a lot of questions, like the good little newspaperman (unpublished novelist) that I am.

<<Tuesday July 25>> *I'm barely staying on top of my earning responsibilities. They seem to pale in importance next to the power of friendship and death and mystery. The looming empty spaces that once were filled with Randall, Bridget, Emily—they randomly open up like holes under my feet and I fall into darkness for a while. Or Siri and I take turns sitting with Ethan, reading Dr. Seuss' Fox in Socks until he giggles, helping him assemble Lego cities, stroking his hair until he sleeps. Or I run searches and make calls, attempting to learn more about Noel Nachtmann. No luck. The name matches I'm turning up don't jibe with this man's story. Also, there appears to have been no former marriage by Bridget's mother. I'm assembling my notes in anticipation of presenting*

them to the hospital and Child Protective Services. I want to block this adoption, but then I ask myself, to what end?

<<Wednesday July 26>> It was Siri who brought up the question we'd both been asking ourselves: could we adopt Ethan? We talked it over across the kitchen table this morning after Sophie went to her day camp. We estimated increased expenses, speculated about ways to increase income, predicted a future of emotional difficulty that would require therapy, acknowledged that the final decision was up to the state, and then we asked each other what we wanted. Later, when Sophie came home, we sat her down with us and asked her how she'd feel about having a little brother. Her face lit up. The vote was unanimous.

<<Thursday July 27>> Today I started the application process to adopt Ethan. It's a long and complicated affair in which we need to prove to the state that we are a nice, happy family with the means to give little Ethan a good life. No problem, we can prove that.

Interesting that I have not run into Noel Nachtmann again. I asked at the nurse's station and they said he got called back to California for a few days but would return soon. Sounds like bullshit to me. I think he knew I was on to him so he won't be coming back. But who is he really? A pervert, a procurer? Why would he want to take Ethan?

<<Friday July 28>> Dedicated to catching up on professional obligations.

<<Saturday and Sunday July 29-30>> I took Siri and Sophie for a getaway to our friend Carol's cabin up in Woodland Valley in the Catskills. Carol is in Europe for the summer and wants an occasional check-in on her cabin, and we needed some relaxation. It was a pleasant two days of taking walks in the woods and lounging around the little stone patio surrounded by wildflowers.

<<Monday July 31>> This will be Ethan's last week in the hospital. As I understand, he will then become a ward of the state and be placed with a foster family until adoption arrangements

*can be made. Siri and I plan to do our best to meet every require-
ment.*

*Over the last week and a half I've been keeping pretty busy
but still noticed that Ben Rose didn't call me to assist with his film
research like he said he would. Normally I would just shrug off
something like this, but his story had a grip on me that wouldn't let
go. This morning, I called his office. A woman answered—his wife,
I assumed—and I asked for Ben. The line was silent for a moment,
then her voice was unfriendly. "Who is this?"*

*"My name is Paul Auster. I met Ben over a week ago and he
was going to call me for help on his film. I never heard from him,
so I'm following up."*

"What day did you see him?" Still no warmth.

*I was taken aback by her demeanor. "It was, uh, Thursday, the
20th."*

*"What time, and where were you?" Clearly, I was being inter-
rogated. Was something going on that I didn't know about?*

"Excuse me, is this Ben's wife? Is everything okay?"

*"Yes, this is Cate. I don't know you, so I'd rather not say more.
But I need you to tell me when and where you last saw Ben."*

*"Hmm, well..." I didn't want to respond to this rudeness. I was
feeling both alarmed and pissed off.*

"Seriously. Please."

*"It was in the afternoon, about 2 p.m., in Kingston, on
Delaware Avenue. We talked a bit and he left. He said he was going
to the Ponckhockie Union Congregational Church over on Abruyn
Street."*

"Can you spell that street name?"

"Wait, it seems like something's very wrong. Can you tell me—"

"I can't say more. Thanks." She hung up on me.

*<<Tuesday August 1>> I can only infer from Ben's wife's
behavior that he is missing from home, perhaps since the day I
saw him. I remember he mentioned his suspicions of her, but would
he just leave without saying anything? What about his daughter?
Maybe I'm intruding on private family stuff. None of my business.*

But the thought keeps nagging: what if he's in trouble? What if that business card prank was a precursor to some unpredictable foul play?

<<Wednesday August 2>> *My beer-bellied detective friend Vince Peluso of the Kingston Police Department is a smart man, circumspect, not a blabber, but he trusts me. When I told him my concerns about Ben Rose and gave him a description, I expected a joking dismissal. Instead, he took a long stare at the floor. Then he looked up at me and said, "This is strictly off the record, Paul. I'm going to show you some photos that were shot yesterday on a little overgrown road in the woods, down by the river in East Kingston."*

Out of a file folder he pulled a stack of 8×10 color prints. What had once been a small hatchback car was completely incinerated, burned to a black hulk. There was no way to know its original color, but my heart sank as I recognized the shape of Rose's Hyundai. Vince said, "We're trying to trace the car, but the plates were removed and the VIN was even filed off. This was a professional job."

Then he set aside the car shots to reveal more photos. My breath stopped and my stomach rolled over as I saw a human shape curled in fetal position on the rear seat, burnt black as coal, nothing but a cinder skeleton. Jaw hanging open, eye sockets empty.

"So far, we know nothing about who this was. No ID near the scene. Due to the position of the body and the destruction of bone, we can't get even get a reliable height for the victim. There's one local missing persons report that we're looking into now, nothing conclusive yet. We've just begun the process of getting DNA samples run and comps made, but it takes time. Weeks."

"Wow. I have to sit down."

Vince got me a cup of cold water while I sat glassy-eyed and mute.

"So...," he said. "You think this might be your friend Ben Rose?"

A sip of water helped calm the nausea rising up in my throat.

The stippled pattern on the floor tiles swam as my mind refused to accept yet another tragedy.

"Oh, god. Fire," I heard myself groan. "Another car fire. He told me a bunch of fire stories; maybe he felt it coming." But as I said it, it didn't sound true.

"Tell me more," Vince said. "Did someone want him dead? Because this was an execution."

I breathed deep and sat up straight. "I don't know. I just met him; I really know nothing about his life."

"You mentioned his wife. I'll need to talk to her, see if I can get a DNA sample."

"Wait. Let me talk to her first; maybe I'm misunderstanding the whole thing." It wasn't adding up for me. Did he foresee his own death? I don't rule out prescience, but skepticism is my guide. And he certainly didn't seem the criminal type, but you never know. More investigation is always good.

"Vince, let's make a trade," I said. "I'll keep a gag on this from a news point of view; you give me a couple of days to see if I can learn more. Deal?"

"Deal."

<<Thursday August 3>> I got Ben's home number from directory assistance. I called his wife seven times today. Four at the office, three at home. Nothing but answering machines every time. I left a message on each. Maybe tomorrow I'll take a drive to Jersey City, but right now the phone is ringing. Who is calling so damned late?

That was the end of the pages Paul had given me, and of course, I knew immediately: the phone ringing was me, finally free.

CAMERA OBSCURA

16: DARKNESS

In the church, I took a step toward the altar, Spanda behind me. Then a touch on the back of my neck and I was simply gone, no memories of falling nor of anything that happened next... until an unknown amount of time later, when I woke up in darkness.

I was in a cool place. It felt good on my skin after the sweltering heat of the day, but I knew that this was not what should be happening. I was lying on what seemed to be a foam pad, curled on my side, a small pillow under my head. My eyes were open but I saw nothing. Very gradually, I stirred, I looked around, and I saw a spot of light in the darkness. Was it the moon, millions of miles away, or something just a few feet above me? As I moved, something about the muffling of the sound gave me the sense I was in a small room. I got to my knees, then to my feet. My sandals and watch were gone but I was still wearing my cargo shorts and loose shirt. I reached out my hands and felt something like cement, both smooth and pebbly. I followed the cement wall with my palms and discovered I was in a space no bigger than a closet, perhaps as big as the inside of my Hyundai, but taller, much higher than my head. There was a hole the size of a nickel at approximately chest height, through which now I saw a beam of light streaming. It was behaving like those Renaissance rooms, a Latin term I couldn't remember, where a tiny hole projected images from outside onto an inside wall. It was just murky shapes and shadows, impossible to make out.

"Hey!" I yelled. "Hey, what the fuck!"

My voice echoed in the small room. Then I heard sounds through the hole and saw a vaguely human-shaped shadow, upside down, growing larger on the wall and I understood it to be someone approaching the hole from the other side. I heard Lester Spanda's voice.

"Mr. Rose, I offer you my humblest apologies."

"What the hell is going on?" I said.

"You see, I had no choice. I could not take the chance of letting you leave."

"So you *are* Jack Dunne," I said. He ignored me.

"I have locked you in a cavity in the wall of the church, which was part of the air cooling system from the 1800s. I need you to stay here. I will take care of you. You will be safe, and perhaps I can even teach you something you might need to know."

"Are you crazy? You're a crazy man!" I yelled. "Help! Help!"

"Mr. Rose, you are in a part of the church that is in the rear, behind several walls. And anyway there's no one here and I don't expect anyone until Sunday. I suggest you relax, make the best of the situation. Let me know if you need food or water. If you need to relieve yourself, I will pass you a bucket. And this is how we will conduct ourselves until further notice. See? No problem."

The guy was completely insane. Why had I met two of them in one week? I decided I needed to be very calculating, not do or say anything alarming. If this was Jack Dunne, he was a cold-blooded killer. I had to make sure I stayed alive. I had to get back home somehow.

"Okay, Spanda... actually, I would love a drink of water."

"Les, Les—call me Les! Haha! Is less more, or less? I choose less, haha!"

"Okay Les, will you please give me a drink of water?"

"Coming right up, sir."

A minute later, I heard a clicking latch and a rusty hinge. At the bottom of the wall below the hole, a door about two feet square creaked open, into my cell. A shaft of light peeked in but was mostly blocked by his body. His hand reached through and gave me a cold bottle of spring water. When I took the bottle from his hand, he immediately pulled the door shut. Closed, there was not even a crack of light around its edges.

I tried to gauge what I could see through the little hole, but the wall was apparently a foot thick, and the hole was at the peak of a cone-shaped recess that widened to eight inches at the inside surface. I could not put my eye up to the hole. I could only see a tiny circular view of a part of a room. No matter how much I moved around for a different angle, I could only see a portion of an opposite wall, on which hung a shirt on a hook and a black and white photo in a thin frame, of what appeared to be an elderly man.

"Mr. Rose..."

"How do you know my name?"

"If you check your pockets, you'll find that you are not carrying your wallet. I also have your possessions from your car, and have taken the liberty of moving your car off the street to a more secure place. Have no fear, it will not be damaged."

"Who is it that you're afraid of?" I said. "Why can't you let me leave? Because I know your secret?"

"Well it's a long story and as a matter of fact, this is a good time to tell it, don't you think? Would you like to relax and listen?"

I thought: whatever keeps him calm. "Okay," I said.

"Also, Mr. Rose, I have taken the liberty of removing the tape from your video camera. I have carefully placed it back in the bag, and have put a new tape in the camera, because I want to tell my story on video. I would like to borrow your camera to do that. Is that okay with you?"

I thought, Wow, here's a guy who's going to confess to kidnapping and who-knows-what other crimes, right on video.

I said, "Sure, if that's what you want to do. If you need help operating it, just ask me."

"Oh no, I'm good with this sort of thing." I heard some rustling and clicking and I assumed he was setting the camera up and inserting a tape. I could not see him but his voice came through the hole quite clearly. "First, Mr. Rose, please clarify where you think we met?"

"Well, someone who looked exactly like you but called himself Jack Dunne, or Mad Dog Dunne, was one of the leaders on a desert survival adventure in southern Utah that I went on with my girlfriend...." He stayed silent, so I continued. "I was a beginning filmmaker at the time and was offered the opportunity to document the event. But I was only there the first three days of a ten-day trip. I left and went back home to New Jersey."

"And what year would you say that was?"

"I'm pretty sure that was the summer of 1975," I said.

I heard the sound of him sitting down in a creaking chair. He added an extra dramatic flair to his voice, a thespian on stage. "Well, sir, here we go! I have just turned on the camera, and I am going to tell you my story."

17: LESTER

"My name is Les Spanda now, but once I was known as Jack Dunne... Mad Dog Dunne, soldier of fortune!

"Ah, yes, the seventies... in those days there were certain secret, powerful circles amongst whom I had a good reputation. I was reliable, efficient. Very very focused. So I got a call one day requesting my presence at a meeting in California, at which I learned that there was a certain Middle Eastern leader who had grown, um... inconvenient. I was being asked to take out Yasser Arafat, Mr. PLO. Well, I gave it some thought, of course, what else would a reasonable man do? And I said yes.

"So that was the last summer, that summer when you were there, the kid with the fancy camera—yes, I remember. That was the last summer I worked with Clay Porter and his people doing teenage excursions in the deserts of Utah. After that I was on a different track, forever.

"Make no mistake, the people who hired me had real influence. I had been, shall we say, a little indiscreet in previous years, so they arranged a cover story by which I could disappear. According to the press, shortly after you and I met, I was tried and convicted for weapons smuggling and sent to prison. Haha!

"That first meeting, in LA, the guys I met with said they were from the Jewish Defense League, but of course they weren't, as I found out later. There were two Middle Eastern men who claimed to be Israeli but were actually Palestinian, and there was another chap, perhaps an American, maybe

European, I never really knew because he didn't speak. I don't really remember his face… very average, tall-ish and slender… but he just sat there without a word, without an expression, through the entire discussion. Gave me the creeps, truly.

"Actually, I saw this fellow again, two more times in fact. Once was near the end of my involvement with these people, during a short stay in Cairo. I just glimpsed him at a distance in what appeared to be a meeting with a few of the PLO leaders, but not Arafat. And then one final time, many months later… I can't be absolutely sure, because by that time he had begun to fade from my memory, but… I was in India, and I saw a television broadcast about a meeting between Israeli and American diplomatic teams. As the camera surveyed the American entourage, I was quite sure I saw him there amongst the other suits and Secret Service types. I never knew his name.

"By the way, a man in my position is a technician—a valuable one, but still just labor. Not management. Information is strictly "need to know." I was told nothing, but naturally I assumed in the beginning that my employers were Israeli, possibly even the government of Israel. But then, by sly observations and inferences, I gleaned that, no, it was Arafat's own people betraying him—a couple of high-up guys whose allegiance was really with Black September, and they were angry that Arafat had shut them down. They feared he was just not militant enough, and after his speech to the UN in, um… autumn of '74, they decided he had to go. His famous statement about the olive branch versus the freedom fighter's gun… ha! They didn't want to hear about an olive branch at all. They were afraid that Arafat would betray their aims and actually bring peace. They were too full of hatred for that. Or so it appeared to me—but that still wasn't the whole picture.

"So… we planned and arranged for several months, and

I was eventually allowed some contact with the Fatah inner circle, posing as a sympathetic British journalist writing a book—your basic Mission Impossible act. You remember the TV series, right? I studied the movements of Mr. Arafat, with the help of my contacts. He was careful, he moved place to place, but finally, in Cairo, I spotted my window of opportunity. It was a middle-of-the-night, classic ninja-style operation, and I was damned good, if I say so myself. I won't go into detail, but I did it—I personally brought the end of life on this temporal plane to the being that was Mr. Yasser Arafat. With my own two hands.

"Then I ducked into hiding, in a place of my own choosing, unknown to my handlers—my fail-safe plan. I had been paid the first two-thirds of my rather hefty fee, so I wasn't handicapped, I could move. I expected a sudden explosion in the press: celebration on one side, mourning on the other. But imagine my surprise when Mr. Arafat appeared just two days later on television. Live.

"Well, clearly something was going on that I didn't know about. That's how these people work, you know. They make sure the right hand does not know what the left hand is doing. Of course, there is somebody somewhere who knows what both hands are doing. But we don't know who that is.

"There was one chap, one of my secret handlers, that I managed to kidnap and threaten with his life, to the point that he gave me more information. I learned that I had seen only one small part of the plot all along. The bigger plan was to replace the real Arafat with an impostor.

"And as it turns out, I was wrong in more ways than one. The people I was working for were not dedicated to Palestinian liberation at all costs, nor to the destruction of the Jews, nor any such thing. Matter of fact, they were traitors to the Arab cause, real Benedict Arnolds, but worse. They were just plain greedy... man's number one weakness, right?

"They were not Black September but they didn't work

for Israel, either. There was some shadowy third party playing one side against the other. Like Israel, they did not want a Palestinian martyr; that would be too hard to handle. But they did want a stronger anti-Israel stance. More terrorist attacks, which of course would be answered with extreme prejudice by the IDF. On and on, back and forth, like it still is all these years later....

"Who knows—maybe Arafat could have brought peace in the Middle East. Imagine that! Maybe it did happen in a parallel universe somewhere, but not here. You're probably thinking: Why? Why did these people want this? Perhaps to ensure the endless riches that come with endless war, for an elite few. Maybe just for power, plain and simple. Who are they? I suspect they are the people who still run the world today.

"Anyway, they had a solution to their problem. They found an Iranian guy, an actor who resembled Arafat. He was an Islamic zealot, I was told, passionate and theatrical. His name was Bijan Zaimi. Maybe he felt chosen by Allah, but he got rich in any case. They did a little plastic surgery on him, spent months rehearsing him, preparing him. The day after I did my job, Arafat's body was disposed of thoroughly, Zaimi took his place, and nobody but a handful of people knew what happened.

"Oh, they were smart. If you have a good memory, you might even remember that there was a news story about a guy named Abu Sa'ed, a Palestinian agent who'd been working for the Mossad for several years. Apparently he was enlisted to put poison pellets that looked like rice in Arafat's food. But after he got the go-ahead, he came forward and confessed. Said he couldn't do it because he was first of all a Palestinian and his conscience wouldn't let him.

"Lies, all lies. This was just a smokescreen, a way to discredit any suspicions, always an effective technique for hiding covert operations. Happened just a week after the big switcheroo, and was an excuse for Arafat to lay low for a while. So... to this day, Zaimi is still parading around in character, as far as I know. Got married, soon to be a father, etc etc. Unless they switched him again—haha!

"But... let's see, where was I?

"Oh yes... suddenly I was one of the few who knew the truth. That meant I was in danger of immediate execution. I left my informant, shall we say, indisposed, and took off. Never to return.

"I wanted to do whatever they didn't think I would do, so I headed east. It was slow going and damned stressful, but I eventually made my way to India—Bombay. You might be surprised at how well I can blend in, live, travel in the darker-skinned countries, make my way through their slums and market places, a big pale Brit like me... I've done it much of my life.

"So I was in Bombay, and some weeks went by and I felt pretty safe there so I decided I would stay—ha! I mean, who would do that? I would. There I was in the heart of steamy, grimy Bombay, hiding in a little hovel in a maze of streets that would be called a slum in any western city. But it was far nicer than the real Bombay slums, where thousands of people live in cardboard shacks on polluted riverbanks or between highway interchanges. I walked the streets, talked to people, occasionally visited the Colaba district down at the southern tip of the city, but mostly avoided that because there were too many tourists and expats and people like me. Too dangerous.

"Anyway, as chance would have it—do you believe in chance? haha!—I learned of a holy man who lived not far away in an attic above a smoke shop, Khetwadi 10th Lane. He was said to be one of the truly enlightened. So I decided to check him out.

"Now as you might guess from my church job today, I've always been deeply interested in spiritual truths. When I was in Utah, I joined the LDS Church, and had I not been given my big opportunity, maybe I'd still be there. A happy Mormon guy with a family—ha!

"You see, I'm devout. Bhakti yoga, my friend—the path of devotion. I'm a naturally religious man. It's in my genes. I come from a long line of religious men, men of vision, men of the cloth. My father was vicar of a small country parish, my mother the daughter of an Anglican deacon. I loved the ritual, the fancy vestments—was even an altar boy, briefly, before the trouble. Jesus was the hero of my bedtime stories. Love, forgiveness and all that. But that doesn't mean we ignored the Old Testament, oh no—fire and brimstone have their place. And fierce was the belt on my backside, or the backhand across my face, if I spoke my own opinion! Both my parents abhorred a spoiled child. And I hated control, so we parted ways, the usual story. But still... something deep in me always sought after the transcendent stories, the secret truths. I always wanted to worship, to kneel at the feet of the beloved, to give my life to service.

"Hmm, perhaps I strayed from the holy path. Or did I? No mortal man knows for sure, haha!

"So... an enlightened guru, right there in my Bombay neighborhood. I wanted to know what he knew. I went up the steep little staircase into his room, which would only hold ten, fifteen people at the most. Crowded, sweaty. When I got there I wasn't even sure which one was him. That's the level of nothingness he had attained. But soon it became evident by the fierceness of his eyes and by the authority with which he spoke. Just a plain, grizzled little guy, bald, no fancy guru robes and such. Just sitting on a deerskin, smoking, coughing, speaking hoarsely. This was Sri Nisargadatta Maharaj. I doubt you've ever heard of him, but he was one of the few truly awake beings in history. Dead now, cancer, 1981. I was long gone by then; I didn't even know he died until years later.

"Anyway, I attended his teaching sessions, twice a week at first, for several months, then later once a week. Then less, as I gained deeper understanding. At first I wasn't sure I was safe, because there were often two or three Europeans, Brits, Americans in the room. Spiritual seekers, yoga pilgrims, ashram-dwellers, you get the picture. Not like me, but that was good. No CIA, no Interpol, no military. No hired killers there but me—haha!

"Nisargadatta's message was very clear, almost brutal, like a slashing sword. Question everything, don't believe in anything. You find out what you truly are by discovering what you are not. Concept by concept, illusion by illusion, you look clearly at it, see it is false, and discard it. *Neti neti*—not this, not this. You peel off the layers of the onion until the only knowledge left is simply: "I am." And then you discard that one as well: No Self. Emptiness. Union with the absolute.

"That is enlightenment. Being fully awake.

"I wanted that. I sat at his feet frequently for the next, oh, many months, maybe even a year. I meditated daily. I grew ever closer to the full realization of truth. I could feel it coming, haha! And there would be glimpses, but then... nope, sorry. It was just so easy to slip back into the illusion, the illusion of myself, my big old egotistical self.

"Still, today, I'm working on it, bit by bit, closer and closer.

"Anyway, that was my India journey, a turning point in my life. It was... what, '77 or '78 by then? And I had heard nothing from my pursuers, whoever they might be. I seemed to have outsmarted them... but I knew I could never return to my previous life. I had grown homesick for the western world. So I left Bombay.

"I went home to England but felt strangely lonely there, a new feeling for me. No relationships left with former family or friends. Managed to find a secluded place in the countryside up near Halifax. Beautiful. Y'know, I actually fell in love there, almost got married. But it seemed I had too many secrets, so she changed her mind.

"Ah... well... such are the consequences of one's life decisions.

"At that point I decided it was time to come back to the States. I knew I couldn't go anywhere near my old stomping grounds, so I ended up in New York City, a good place to hide, almost as good as Bombay. But after a year or so, I decided I wanted a little more peace and quiet so I moved to Kingston and found this job.

"I've had so many identities throughout all the years... but of course I know that all of them, even the one I was born with—not Jack Dunne, by the way—are just costumes. When I die—and it may be soon, right? haha!—when I die I'll just throw off the final costume and merge back into the absolute, just be part of the divine pulsation, the great, beautiful throb of creation. That's what 'spanda' means, in Sanskrit. And it is my aim to be truly less and less every day. So I've been known as Lester Spanda ever since I left Bombay. I think it suits me, don't you?"

18: BREATHE

As Spanda told his story, I sat cross-legged in the darkness, staring at the little bright dot on the wall that was the only passageway to the outside world, and I listened. I imagined that Spanda was a schizophrenic, an entirely insane individual, an extremely dangerous lunatic, now holding me captive. I also imagined that he was not crazy at all, that his entire tale was true, and that somehow I had the misfortune of stumbling into something big and dark and twisted.

Both scenarios: bad. In either case, I had to stay entirely focused on one thing: surviving. I needed to get back home.

So when he finished, I answered him: "Sure, Les, I think it suits you just fine."

I calculated that I was not going to be able to physically overpower him in any way. For example, as he handed me something through the door, if I were to try to grab him, force his compliance somehow, I would just end up getting hurt. The man was older than me but strongly built, and—much more important—a trained killer. So it seemed to me that staying calm and talking to him would be the best way to make sure I stayed safe.

"There's one more thing I need to tell you," Spanda said. "Your life is in danger. It was already so, but is even more now that you've come here. I've had other friends besides you that I've told my story, and I regret to say they are no longer with us. I am speaking of my neighborhood friends Randall and Bridget O'Brien...."

He paused and I thought: no, no, I don't want to hear this.

I don't want to know he is involved in their deaths. This will break my mind.

"I met them when they came to the church. We chatted, became friends, they invited me over for dinner. This was just a few weeks ago. Ms. O'Brien was a well-published journalist and I found that she was very skillful at drawing me out, getting me to speak. I ended up telling them the whole story I just told you. I didn't want to, but I did. I can't hold it back, it forces its way out, it's bigger than me. She was very interested in knowing more, and maybe being able to write a book. I told her that may not be a good idea but we can talk about it later...."

He paused again and took a deep breath. I sat in darkness, my head in my hands.

"But... it was not meant to be. Just yesterday, we had the funeral of my friends Randall and Bridget and their little daughter Emily, right here in this church. They had perished in a terrible car fire on Saturday, and their little son is now without a family. It's all a tragedy, and people say it was unforeseeable, an accident, an act of God. But they had become my friends and I had told them my story. It's my fault. This is a coincidence that is *not* a coincidence if you are in the circles that I have been in."

Sitting in my black hole, I had been sinking into despair as he spoke. I thought: oh no, and I'm next. Unless he's totally full of shit. He went on as if he knew my thoughts.

"You were never entirely safe because of my indiscretions in the desert twenty years ago. As a matter of fact, Clay Porter, who knew nothing more than my soldier resumé and my presence in Utah, died young, heart attack at 49. You may remember two of the guides, Jerry Harris and Kent Breszky: dead in a car crash, together. Amy Bennett..."

"Wait!" I said. "Amy Bennett is dead? She was my girlfriend."

"Married, name changed, and no, not dead. She was

struck by a mysterious brain ailment and is in a highly-impaired state, under constant medical care. There was some debate about her life support a few years back."

I had no way to confirm any of this information. I desperately did not want to believe.

"So you see, Mr. Rose, now that you've been here, especially after what I've told you, your life is hanging by a thread. That's why this little room where you are right now is the best place you could possibly be. It's my duty to protect you. No one knows you're here, you can't be heard or seen, and you will be safe."

How could I respond to this? But I needed to keep a dialogue going, I needed to lift my energy and get back in the game.

"Les," I said, keeping a gentle tone, "I appreciate your good intentions, but I hardly feel safe here. You have not given me a reason to feel safe; I'm a prisoner, and I don't know what you're going to do with me. Now that you've told me this, maybe you're the one who will kill me."

"No," he said, "If I had wanted to do that, it would be done."

I said, "How about if I help you take this to the authorities so that we can get some protection from whoever it is that's a threat."

"Nah," he said. "There are no, as you say, authorities, who are immune to the influence of the people that we're talking about."

"And just who *is* that?" I said.

"Well, I don't know their names, I don't know where they live, I don't know where their offices are located, but I promise you they are there, and they are watching, and they are listening, and they are not patient when their interests are threatened."

"Les," I was begging now, "This is not a workable situation we have here. Let me out so we can talk about it."

"I'm sorry, I can't do that. Please settle in as my guest. I will do my best to protect you and at some point there will come a time when you are free to leave my lodgings behind. Just know that what I say is true, Mr. Rose.... Relax into what is the current reality, and perhaps let me share some things with you that may be valuable."

I took a slow breath deep into my lungs. "Look," I said, "Just call me Ben, okay?"

"Now," he said, "Ben... I need to run some errands. I'm going to leave you here and I'm going to give you a makeshift toilet in case you need to relieve yourself."

The little door opened and he slid in a bucket that sloshed with what sounded like a couple inches of water, with a not-unpleasant soapy smell. The door closed with a click and a second click. A moment later, the light in the hole went dim, I heard another door close in the outer room, and I was alone. Alone in utter darkness.

My chest was constricted, heart suddenly palpitating. I had no idea what time it was, but certainly Cate and Ava would be expecting me soon, if not now. They would be sitting at Luigi's and certainly Cate would be getting angry. If hours had passed, they would have gone home, to encounter... what? Was Nils Nilsson, the mystery man, part of all this? I imagined terrible scenarios and told myself I'd seen too many spy movies and assassin movies and I had to stop my imagination. How was I to do that? *How was I to do that?*

The only thing available to me to calm myself was breathing. Cate occasionally took yoga classes, did some yoga at home. She'd taught me some poses and we'd talked about the importance of the breath. So I clung to that now like a drowning man. I breathed in deep, let my breath out slowly. Breathed in deep, let my breath out slowly, focused on emptying my mind of the wild imaginings, speculations, the terror. Breathe deep, let it out slowly. Breathe deep, let it out slowly.

I guessed maybe an hour, hour and a half had passed when Spanda came back. "Les," I said, "Can you tell me what time it is?"

"Not important," was his clipped answer.

A wave of fury rose up in me. I wanted to fucking rip him to shreds. But I took a deep breath and didn't say a word.

"Now," said Les. "I know you're angry as hell with me. Who wouldn't be? But I promise you, if you'll pay attention to what I'm going to say, and if you'll participate with me in the training I'm going to give you, your life will benefit. Now, continue the breathing that I know you're doing right now to keep from yelling at me in rage, and I'm going to ask you to follow along with some activities. I know you've been sitting, probably feeling stiff for some time, so this will help work out a few kinks, get you back in your body. First, if you're sitting, stand up."

I continued to sit. I did not want to play kindergarten games with this madman.

"Come, my friend, your body will be grateful. Please stand."

Holding only to the need to please him for my survival, I clambered to my feet, touching a cool cement wall in the darkness.

"Stretch your arms as high as they'll stretch. First one, then the other. Trust me."

I stretched, and it felt good. I continued following his instructions.

"Bend slowly down at the waist—be careful not to bump your head on the wall—and hang. Let your head hang, your arms hang, let your shoulders and neck relax, breathe in...... breathe out...... breathe in...... then as you breathe out, slowly slowly raise yourself up. Curl your backbone up, one vertebra at a time, up to the vertical position, until your neck is straight again. Now, repeat that routine as you listen to me. I'm going to say a little about what I learned from my beloved Sri Nisargadatta Maharaj."

I did as he said, taking my time, feeling the muscles, stretching up, right side, left side, up, up, then gradually folding at the waist, hanging head and arms, breathing, hanging, then slowly slowly up again. He kept speaking.

"First… everything—you, me, this church, the whole universe—is made of just one substance, one essence. We might call that one substance consciousness or awareness, or the quantum field. I don't know if these things are exactly the same, but the point is, all of the millions of differentiated objects that we see, or even think of, are all just various condensations of that one substance.

"So that's the first thing, the fundamental thing. The ancient Indian sages understood this, and they called their philosophy Advaita: 'not two.'

"Second… to find out who or what you are, you must first find out who you are not. What you know about yourself came from outside of you, therefore discard it. So anything you *think* you are, you are not. *Neti neti*: not this, not this. The real you is beyond anything that can be known with the mind."

Fuck you and your guru too, I thought. But still, my muscles wanted this. Now I was bent again at the waist, my head upside down, my arms dangling, my shoulders and neck relaxing into gravity's pull. My physical body, its sensations, had to be my link to sanity in this insane situation. He went on.

"Third… question everything; do not believe anything.

"Fourth… the only thing you can say about yourself—say with absolute truth—is 'I am.' Let go of everything else. Just hold to that. Hold to that.

"Now, here's a perfect bit of wisdom from Nisargadatta to you, Ben Rose. I quote: 'The door that locks you in is also the door that lets you out. The "I Am" is the door; stay at it until it opens. As a matter of fact, it is open, only you are not at it. You are waiting at the non-existent painted doors, which will never open.'"

I was tempted to blurt, "Well, if I should question everything, I question that! I am obviously a prisoner here, you asshole!" But I didn't speak, I just stretched.

"Meditate on what I've told you," Spanda said. "And in the morning, we'll do more." He went quiet, and stayed quiet. I heard an occasional rustle, the scrape of a chair leg on the floor, and sometime later faint sounds that I thought might be the pages of a book, infrequently turning.

I sat cross-legged for a long time. I breathed. I lay down.

My mind was obsessive, repetitive: over and over, I imagined Cate and Ava worrying, wondering where I was, afraid I was dead or had abandoned them. Cate would be angry along with her worry. My darling little Ava would pick up the vibes from Cate and just be innocently full of sadness and fear. I visualized scenes of their distress, again and again with different settings and details. Their terror, their tears.

With these thoughts came boiling rage. I wanted to kill Spanda. I'm sure some men in my situation would succumb to anger; would rant and pace and yell. Break their knuckles punching a wall. That's not my style. I had to think my way out of this, use reason and facts. The first fact I knew was this: right now, I was powerless. My only way forward was to conserve strength. I needed to stay alert, ready for whatever might happen, ready to jump at any opportunity to escape.

But it had only been a few hours (how many? I didn't know), and I was already beginning to feel disoriented, separated from reality. Under the interminable pressure of unchanging, claustrophobic darkness, I began to drift. I couldn't help myself. In order to survive, I slept.

19: VOID

Deep in the heart of a timeless black silence, I felt that I awoke from a dream. But perhaps the waking was also a dream; I had no way of knowing. I had been running from someone chasing me. At first it was like when I was a boy in JC. My buddies Artie and HueyMac and I had each stolen an apple from an elderly street vendor on Kennedy Boulevard. He chased and we ran, and as I pounded along the street, I was filled with a huge, delirious joy. I laughed as I ran, my body strong and swift and free.

In the dream, I exulted in my freedom as I fled through sunny, empty streets from someone unseen, but before long the feeling changed. My friends were gone. The streets became narrow alleys between windowless walls, and the sky grew low and dark. I gradually realized that I was in mortal danger; that whoever was after me was intent on my death and nothing less. All joy was gone.

Did I awake? It seemed that my eyes were open, but who knows? It didn't matter.

Some time later, I opened my eyes again. Through the tiny bright hole I heard Spanda's voice with a cheery good morning. The bucket came and went, followed by an egg sandwich and a cup of coffee.

At Spanda's urging, and because I knew it would help my body feel better, I got to my feet and did stretching exercises. Spanda began right away with his teachings, his bullshit "wise sage" act. He started by covering the same ground as yesterday, a repeat of his basic principles, almost word for word. Then he went further. Today was a meditation lesson, and at first I resisted. *A murderous maniac teaching meditation!* I snarled inside. *You insane asshole!*

But the gentle friendliness of his voice began to wear me down, and soon I found I was glad to have something, anything, to occupy my mind, to give some relief from the alternating current of useless worry and rage.

I sat as comfortably as I could, eyes closed, and followed his instructions. "As it always does," he said, "a thought appears. Now ask yourself, 'To whom does this thought appear?' The answer of course is 'To me.' Now ask yourself, 'Who is this I?'

"Do it again... To whom does this thought appear? To me. Who is this I? ... And again...."

After several repetitions of that, he gently and patiently went on. "Now, when a thought appears, ask yourself, 'From where does this thought arise?' Then, when it fades away, ask yourself, 'To where does this thought subside?' Don't really try to invent an answer; just observe the empty space. Do it again... and again... and again."

I knew this should be Friday, but nothing felt sure. That morning we went through the meditation exercises over and over... then, some hours later, did it all again.

In between, Spanda was gone and I was alone. I napped, I stretched, I half-heartedly tried the meditations, I sent mental messages to Cate and Ava, I once again ran my fingers around the edges of the door but could find nothing to grip, not even a crack. Later, he fed me again and I was grateful.

When he woke me for the next lesson, I had no sense of time. I felt detached from my body and thought it must be the middle of the night and he had the light on in his room. We started again from the beginning: Advaita... what you are not... question everything... I Am. We went through the meditations again... from where does this thought arise? And then he added more.

"Now," he said, "without using thought, memory, emotion, association, perception, attention, or intention... are you a man, a woman, or neither?"

My first reaction was *Gimme a fuckin' break*, but then I felt the challenge of the first part of the question, the call to reject normal thinking, to find some deeper way of non-habitual being. Was it possible?

He kept going: "Without using thought, memory, emotion, association, perception, attention, or intention... are you perfect, imperfect, or neither? And... without using thought, memory, emotion, association, perception, attention, or intention... what does the word 'perfect' even mean?"

On and on he went, defying every tenet of everyday living. "Without using thought, memory, emotion, association, perception, attention, or intention... are you worthless, worthy, or neither? What does 'worth' even mean?"

Alone, connected, or neither? Capable, incapable, or neither? Do you exist, not exist, or neither? What does "existence" even mean? Without using thought, memory, emotion, association, perception, attention, or intention, what does anything mean? What concept or preconceived idea can remain in the path of that cleansing fire?

I saw that every time I genuinely tried to let go of all those ingrained mental structures, there was no answer to any question. There was only a blank space, a tiny void. And then the mind came swarming in again.

Spanda's voice continued. "Ben, with these exercises you have now observed what we might call the 'stateless' state or the 'no-state' state, the little emptiness of no thought. Now let's do one more thing... first, become aware of that no-state state. Then allow awareness to expand outward or fall backward, and notice the big emptiness that goes on forever."

I heard and I followed, but maybe I was out of my depth,

drowning... I was lost in some liquid space without up or down. He kept speaking.

"And finally, notice what happens if the one who is aware of the emptiness and the emptiness are made of the same substance."

I must have cried out as I spun in some sort of vertigo. Spanda's voice was gentle. "Ben, you'll be okay. Rest now. We'll continue another time."

Time. It passed, or not. I slept and woke and slept, ate occasionally, listened to Spanda repeating my lessons, and practiced finding the big emptiness. It was there, I glimpsed it, but I could never stay for long. Memories from my life flooded in, full of detail and emotion, and I had vivid dreams of all sorts, so real I once cried real tears when I awoke from Cate's arms into my black prison cell.

My plan had been to wait until Sunday when people would be at church, and then yell my head off to get their attention. But now I wasn't interested in that course of action. Anyway, I had lost track of what day it was. Why did it matter?

*

In all the years since, I have told very few people about these events. One reason for my reluctance is embarrassment. I felt ashamed of how quickly I crumbled, how vulnerable I was to the simplest of brainwashing techniques, how easily I could have become a Stockholm Syndrome statistic.

When I tell about it, I always abbreviate, I always skim the surface. There is no way language can capture the actual experience. The words that some of my Woodstock friends have reflected back to me are these: "spiritual awakening."

I reject that term. "Spiritual" is too vague, too multiplicitous. I don't know what it means. Perhaps "awakening" applies, if viewed from years later. But in 1995, the result was not awakening, it was disintegration. It was a disassembly, a slow combustion. It turned me to ash.

20: DESERT

At one point, I lay curled on my side in the blackness, knowing full well that my hold on reality was slipping far, far away. Spanda's (Dunne's?) voice still seemed to drone in my ears, and it reeled me back twenty years to that Utah experience when I met him, to more memories, things I had long forgotten, things I suddenly needed to remember.

But this was more powerful than just a memory. I was actually there, reliving it all.

It was early morning and I was in the foreign town of Provo. Four days earlier I had left here with a few counselors and a sullen group of juvenile delinquents on a desert survival trek, a court-mandated therapeutic experience. They were still deep in the desert, but I had been on the job to document the trip on film, and now I had to return to everyday life while they trekked on for another week. I had been there just for the initiation, the sudden plunge into hardship, the slap of reality on the faces of the overfed, those first three days that are called "impact." We had caravanned in cars south from Provo four hours, to the top of Boulder Mountain, where we had camped the first night on the edge of a beautiful pine-covered plateau. Around a fire in the blue dusk we sang and told stories, but then came the first night of poor sleep, shivering on hard ground, under the open sky. The morning was fresh and sweet, perfect to launch us on the interminable walking that came next. There were no high-tech sleeping bags, no fancy backpacks, no Gore-Tex pants or Patagonia pullovers. Each of us had an army-blanket bedroll in which we carried an extra set of stocks, shirt, and jeans. I carried more—cameras and film.

And for food, each of us had nothing but a sandwich bag full of "gorp"—nuts, dried fruit, and chocolate chips. Far more important was the canteen of water we each carried, for we were now descending from the piney mountain into the vast labyrinth of desert canyons that we had looked down upon from our campsite. As we walked steadily downhill the ground changed from dark pine-needle-covered soil to dry sand and stone. The tall, straight lodgepole pines, with their rough, reddish bark and long-needled tufts on high, spare, elegant branches, gradually thinned out and disappeared, replaced by occasional scraggly cedars, low clumps of cactus, and the blades and stalks of yucca. The air grew hot and parched, no more moist scent of pine.

For three long days, it felt like there was nothing but walking, as if the entire world was reduced to the rhythmic motion of putting one foot in front of the other, over and over and over. Eyes had to stay on the trail, the stones, the cactus, the heels of the walker in front. Eyes down as the sun broiled the top of the head, the shoulders, the nose. Gratitude for the rare small running streams where we could fill our canteens, after the warnings about the alkaline puddles in the shade of boulders, whose liquid could make you deathly ill. Long periods of no voices, just the rustle of bedrolls, thump of boots, clank of canteens. And then little explosions of anger, shoving, arguments between kids who didn't want to be there, intercessions by the counselors sometimes calm and strong, sometimes wisecracking, and then the return to walking, walking.

I had to do my job. I was hungry and tired, but I had to break ranks, hurry ahead, frame a shot of the line of hikers, try to slow my heart and breath to get a steady hand-held shot with my 16-millimeter camera, then join the walk again.

The first night, everyone was silent, too exhausted to speak. We rolled up in our blankets and slept. The second day, relationships began to change. Some people were strong, some were weak. Where there had been conflict there began to be helping. When a girl twisted her ankle, two guys walked beside her, her arms around their shoulders. I attempted to get it all on film, but I felt I was failing. I did not want the responsibility. I wanted to leave the camera under a rock and just focus on my own experience, the meditation of walking, the sores on my feet, my sunburn, my thirst, my hunger. The desolate beauty all around.

We were like a family with three levels of experience amongst us: the dozen teenagers who had never done anything like this were the babies; the three counselors, including Amy, were the older siblings—twenty-somethings like me but who, unlike me, had been on such trips several times already; and at the top, the father figure, a man named Clay who was near forty, had a wife and kids, and ran these excursions as part of his job with a social services agency. Clay was tall and fit, with thinning brown hair and a calm, capable demeanor. He knew how to defuse tension with a gentle joke, and he knew this labyrinth of desert canyons as well as I knew the streets of my neighborhood. He was a trustworthy leader.

And then there was the cool, weird uncle: Jack Dunne, a perfectly integrated member of the family with his buddy-buddy demeanor, world-traveled authority, and movie-spy skills.

I didn't fit. I was an outsider, added in at the last minute. Too old for the rank and file, too inexperienced for leadership, and often resented by people who didn't want their picture taken. I had no choice but to do my job, worried every minute that the omnipresent sand was getting into the workings of my camera and lenses and into the canisters of film. At rest stops and in campfire light I obsessively used my little soft brush and bulb-like air blower to clean the grains of sand from everything.

I thought, if only I didn't have this job to do, I could enjoy this. This harsh, wild beauty, this journey to the limit of myself. What had I been thinking? I did not want to be a filmmaker after all. I just wanted to be a person alive, facing the elemental human needs: food, water, movement, comfort, relationships. I loved this alien landscape and gradually, even these alien people. But it was coming to an end.

The third day was blessedly cloudy, the brutal eye of the sun no longer blasting us, but the flat white ceiling adding to the sense of unreality as we straggled through a long dry canyon of gray stone and soft gray dirt, barren sky, barren land, and there seemed a strange new depth of silence in the air, no birds, no animals, a muffled, solemn, deathly place.

I shot no film that day. I told myself the light was bad, no shadows, too dull, too ugly. I didn't care.

Like everybody else, I had no food left. We walked in silence, we stopped, drank from our canteens, stared at the ground, got up and walked again. One thing kept all of them going: the knowledge that at the end of this day, the impact phase would be over and a big delicious meal awaited them, followed by a full day of rest. For me it was the knowledge that my job was done, I was going home. It was late afternoon when we emerged from the canyon of death at the same time that long low rays of sunshine broke through under the cloud blanket, and there before us was a river, a scattering of greenery, some cottonwood trees, and a soft-sand beach perfect for a campsite. This was our destination, and there were whoops of joy as everybody ran to the water, dropping their bedrolls, shedding shoes, wading in, splashing faces.

I knew I should get this on film, but first I had to feel and taste the water myself, and then it was too late. I missed the whole scene and I didn't really care.

Another member of Clay's staff had brought in food before we arrived, and a feast was about to be prepared. As the fire was being built, Clay said to me, "Ready to go?" This was our plan—at the end of impact, he and I would leave. I had to go back to my real job; he had to check in on his family. He would return to the desert after a couple of days and switch again with the other leader, to bring the group to the end of their ten-day adventure.

I took a deep breath, went to that well-cultivated place in me that demanded endurance to the bitter end, that didn't allow complaint, and told him, "Yes, let's go."

We said quick goodbyes and I felt no blame that everyone was more focused on dinner and relaxation than on us. Besides, they were entertained by Dunne and his antics with explosives as Clay and I took off walking. Walking. Again. We didn't speak, we just hiked. Uphill, once again into pines, and the dusk was deep by the time we arrived at the agency vehicle, a pickup truck parked at a ranger station. I was surprised at how close we had been to civilization—camp had seemed the most remote, wild place, and only a couple of miles away was a building, a phone, people.

But not now; night had fallen and we were alone there. In the cab of the truck were two quart cans of tomato juice and a can opener. We each opened a can and guzzled the most delicious liquid meal I could ever remember having. It felt like life returning to my tissues, my cells, as I drank.

Then with Clay driving, we headed for home on a dirt road, a shortcut across the high plateau of Boulder Mountain. I watched the trees and brush slide by in the headlights until my eyes just had to close and, grateful to no longer be walking, I drifted into exhausted sleep.

Suddenly I was jarred awake, flung hard against the door. Thumps and bangs filled my ears. I opened my eyes, heart pounding, to see only sagebrush and shadows in the pitching headlights as we bounced across rocks to a lurching stop. Clay groaned, "Oh man, I'm sorry, I fell asleep."

"Do you need me to drive?" I said, dreading the answer.

"No, no, I'm awake now." He started the truck up again and steered back onto the road. Again I watched the moving pool of light on the rutted road until I fell like a stone into unconsciousness.

But then it happened again. Sudden panic, clawing its way to my awareness, as the truck banged over brush and stones. I bounced like dice in a cup, delirious, hallucinating, couldn't tell if I was awake or asleep, alive or dead. I didn't know if there were cliffs or trees in our path or how fast we were going or if in the next moment I would be torn in two.

"Oh shit, oh shit, damn it to hell!" I heard Clay blurt out, Clay who was a Mormon and never swore. This time he steered back onto the road without stopping and we kept going, alive by miracle only. His unspoken apology hung in the air—twice! almost killed!—but I couldn't demand to drive, I couldn't rise to that duty, it was entirely beyond me. My exhaustion was bone-deep, an utter paralysis. I was trapped with nowhere else to go.

All I could do was try my hardest to stay awake because I did not want to die. Or if I was to die that night, I wanted to see it coming. At some point we made it to a paved highway and although I struggled mightily against sleep, everything else is gone from my memory except one more moment: Clay was muttering and I rose to consciousness to see that we were cruising slowly through a herd of deer, maybe twenty, all like shadows standing mute and spectral, clustered along both sides of the dark road, their eyes glowing blue as we crept past.

It was almost dawn when we got back to civilization, the town not yet stirring, the eastern sky a sliver of turquoise. We stopped at the agency offices to pick up my suitcase, then Clay dropped me at the Greyhound station so I could get a bus to the Salt Lake City airport. He drove away and I never saw him again. This was our plan, and I knew already it was a bad one. Why didn't he tell me how fucked-up I'd feel? After all, it was called "impact," right? My body was depleted and I had no one to tell that surely I had almost died, that only by some miracle was I still breathing.

I remember curling in a fetal position on a hard bench in the bus depot, until hunger and thirst dragged me to my feet. I wandered. The town was an alien world, more foreign and meaningless than anyplace I had ever been. I was a voyager returning, but nothing was as it had been just days earlier. The terrible roar of monstrous cars and trucks swarming everywhere, the painfully hard flat surfaces that covered the ground in gray as far as the eye could see, the severe right angles and impossibly straight lines all around me, the shouting assault of signs demanding who-knows-what, the words and letters all incomprehensible hieroglyphics. And most alien of all, the humans with their fresh-scrubbed faces and dead eyes bustling about on their ordered missions, standing in lines, stopping and going according to the alternating color of a light bulb, speaking and gesturing and speaking and speaking without a single syllable of intelligible meaning. It was all an overload of chaos and I just wanted to go back to the desert.

I went on. As I always did, I went on. Sometime later I was on a bus, then in an airport. I writhed with troubled dreams in my narrow seat for hour after hour, then slept again at home. The next morning, still trembly but less dazed, I returned to my job in the print shop. A few days later I picked up my reels of unremarkable film from the lab and put them in the mail to the agency in Utah to use as they pleased. Inside, I beat myself for being unprofessional, a failure as a filmmaker.

Another week went by, and when I spoke to Amy on the phone, she bubbled over about the wonderful experience they had all had—the sweet camaraderie, the depths of self-knowledge gained, the fun, the beauty, the satisfaction of an adventure completed. I was silent, entirely alienated and unable to speak.

In those few days in the desert and that final night journey, I had suffered some type of physical and psychological trauma. I didn't understand it then, but I could not bounce back to the person I'd been before, when I began my relationship with Amy. And so the silence just grew longer and we faded into each other's pasts.

There in my Ponckhockie dungeon, my eyes popped open. I stared at the nothingness, the Source. Out of it came a realization about myself as a result of that experience I had just re-lived. In 1975, when I was just a kid, I had no words for what I had learned. But now I did. I had learned that inside me there is a very deep well of resilience—an ability to let go of things that are not important, in order to survive. In other words, I can say *neti neti*—not this, not this. This is not necessary, nor is this. There is a glowing core, a diamond far underground, under the strata of soil and rock, a kernel of ultimate truth that is simply "I am." I can hold to that, and I can get through anything.

Desperately, in my lightless prison, I clung to that thought.

Today, from the vantage point of yet another twenty years, I see how crucial was that ability to focus on the diamond inside and endure to the end, as it got me through the days and nights of darkness with a shred of sanity left. But in the seventies, at the age of twenty, I had not yet discovered how important it is to embrace our multiple selves. Back then, I viewed that long-suffering part of me as an alarming, dark being, a sour Puritan, a gray-clad Party official, Comrade Tight-ass-ovitch, who insists that the only moral choice is duty, never pleasure. He had ruled far too many of my life decisions. I hated him. I didn't yet know the simple cure: he needs to smile. He needs to be hugged until he melts. He needs to be literally loved to death.

21: CINEMA

The dazzling beauty of the Empire State Building at midnight... I peered through the viewfinder of my 8mm pawnshop movie camera, the most exciting purchase I had ever made. I was fifteen. I was kneeling on the sidewalk, a big cool slab of Catskills bluestone. We were ready to break and run at any moment because the camera was on sticks (newly acquired film lingo meaning "tripod"), and that meant we needed a permit from the NYC Mayor's Office. Slim chance of that.

HueyMac and Artie were positioned at staggered distances ahead, in front of the camera. It was a special-effects shot in which each of them would pop into and out of existence as the city stayed solid around them. I planned to push the film two stops in the lab, and hope that the street lights gave enough foreground illumination. Experimental filmmaking!

Through the viewfinder I could see that HueyMac was not in a good position for my composition. The words formed in my mind, *HueyMac, move a foot to your right, man!* Then, just before I opened my mouth to shout it out to him, he moved exactly a foot to his right.

The shot was beautiful to my eyes, but when I got the film back from the lab it was... dark. Damn.

Try again next week, and again—the three of us wild and free on the streets, smoking a joint on the way to the PATH station, rushing up the subway steps into the Village, our high-tops scuffing the mica-sparkled sidewalks in unison, camera bag on my shoulder, tripod on HueyMac's, little Artie dancing ahead to spout Kerouac word-for-word to every passerby.

We all got high on mescaline the night we went to see the movie *Woodstock*. Artie's older brother had actually been at the concert over a year earlier, but the three of us were "too young." We sat close to the screen, and our minds were suitably blown. Afterward, we slumped into a diner booth to load up on fries and ketchup before heading home.

I looked across the table at HueyMac and sent a thought-beam, a snatch of lyrics we'd just heard, from "Pinball Wizard" by The Who. HueyMac, on the aisle end of the seat, suddenly grinned and, in perfect time with my thought, belted out the line that followed, about the miracle pinball kid, swinging his right arm in a full Pete Townshend windmill on air guitar. We whooped with the power chords reverberating in our ears until people's heads turned.

"Shh, maintain!" Artie hissed.

I did it again. In silence, a thought-beam of a couplet from another verse. And HueyMac, aloud, again in perfect time, yawped the next line, growled the guitar notes—the arm swishing in a big circle, the music thumping in our minds. I framed a shot of him with my fingers. We all guffawed, then hushed. We ate our fries.

That was it. He was catching my thoughts. Or were we all just stoned? Yes, we were. It was funny. We were kids.

But now I was an adult, a middle-aged man, trapped in a dungeon. I lay half-drowned on a midnight beach, awash in wavelets of the fragmented, irrelevant past.

*

At certain times of day it seemed that more light than usual filled the room beyond the wall. That's when my cell became a... a... *camera obscura*, yes, that was it—"dark chamber," a 16th century technology once used as a drawing aid.

It was a giant pinhole camera, the tiny aperture like the pupil of an eye. If Spanda was in his room, I would see a dim image of him cast upon my dark wall, upside down and backwards, moving around like a ghost. I would sit and watch, as if it were a movie projected on a screen. I was reminded of my college philosophy class and Plato's allegory of the cave. In it, people were chained inside a cave, staring at a wall upon which shadows were cast from a fire behind them and other people moving past it, all outside the awareness of the prisoners. For them, the shifting shadows on the wall were reality. They had no knowledge of the light and activity behind them, nor of the big bright world outside the cave. If someone got free, saw the truth, even ventured out into the light of day, and then returned with a message of freedom, no one would believe him. Here I was, like them, a prisoner, but one who has known the outside world. Now, that world was distant, unreal, like a dream dimly remembered. The shifting shadows on the wall had become my actual reality.

I sat there musing, and modernized the parable in my mind: the cave was a movie theater where the audience members were chained to their seats, staring at flickering shapes on a screen, believing those images to be the real world. Hadn't I, film buff since childhood, often thought I could be happy just sitting endlessly in a theater, lost in the fabulous images and stories reeling out across the big screen? But now I didn't want that anymore. No more illusion! I wanted to stand up, walk up the aisle past the projection booth, into the lobby and out the door into brilliant sunlight.

And maybe Lester Spanda was showing me the door.

*

Out of the darkness came a memory of something I hadn't thought of in many many years... a film I had planned in college, based on my Utah adventure. It had been vivid in my mind, but it never went beyond the storyboard stage, just a stack of 5×7 index cards, rubber-banded, one card per shot, with a rough pencil sketch and a few cryptic notes on each: LS for Long Shot, CU for Close-Up, etc.... duration in seconds... SFX for Sound Effects, VO for Voice-Over... and scribbled lines of dialogue. Suddenly now the whole film came back to me with the full force of its original, fully-imagined presence, as if I were twenty again. Shot by shot it splashed across the blackness, and I relived it.....

Fade up on a beautiful image of a harsh but scenic desert, slanting golden sunlight on stone cliffs and a tall butte in the distance. The camera tilts down and we see, near us on the ground, a bedroll, canteen, hat, and a knife in a leather sheath. A boy's stealthy hand creeps into frame, unsnaps the handle, and takes the knife. The sheath is left empty.

The main title appears: SANDSTONE. We hear a man's voice. Dialogue is in progress. "Yeah, these ol' walls are pretty darn tall and strong; seems like they last forever. But anyway, Bennie, this will be your solo area. You've got your whistle, just like everybody else, and I know where you are, but you won't know where I am. So if you need me, and it's something really important, you blow that whistle. Now, use what you've learned, okay?"

As the man speaks, the title goes away and we see a whistle in a teenage boy's hand. The boy, Bennie, looks sullen as he puts the whistle in his t-shirt pocket. The man, Clay, is wearing the hat we saw earlier. When he claps a hand on Bennie's shoulder in friendly reassurance, the boy shrugs it off. He won't make eye contact.

Clay is disappointed, but kind. "Take care, Bennie." He turns and walks away into the desert. Bennie watches him go, and we see that Bennie is looking at the empty scabbard on Clay's belt. Then the boy turns and walks the opposite direction, kicking at the sand in anger.

Next we see Bennie's head and shoulders, apparently

resting on a slab of sandstone. His eyes are closed, and we hear his voice: "They found him dead on the hard stone. He was strong and silent and needed no one."

Then we're back to Bennie walking through the desert. With a sudden movement, he grabs the whistle out of his shirt pocket and throws it. It lands in sand. Then he grasps his canteen and wrenches off the lid. He pours the water out and it splashes on stone, soaks into sand. He tosses the canteen away. Meanwhile we hear his voice again: "Hmm, let's see…. He was dead when they found him, strong and silent as the stone."

Again we see Bennie lying on stone, spread-eagled, face toward the cloudless sky, eyes shut. We continue to hear his thoughts: "The buzzards wheeled through the sky above him, waiting…"

He opens one eye, closes it, sighs. We see the brutal sun above him.

"Come on sun, my water is gone. Dry me up, wither me like a leaf, suck up every drop, bleach my bones to white. Let me drift away like dry old dust, like sand shifting aimlessly in the dunes."

As his thoughts roll out, we see the empty canteen lying on the dry ground and his bedroll dropped in the dirt. He lies, arms outstretched, on a boulder below a rust-colored cliff. But now we see that in Bennie's right fist is the knife, Clay's knife, that we had seen being stolen in the opening shot. It is pointed toward the sky. He bakes under the sun.

Clay's voice is suddenly heard: "Want some water, Bennie?"

Clay appears to be standing over Bennie, reaching out to him a canteen of fresh water. Bennie is now remembering an earlier part of the expedition, when he sat with the other members, resting against a boulder along the trail. He refuses the water, then refuses a hand up as well.

"Okay," Clay shrugs. As he replaces the canteen on a clip

on his belt, Bennie's eyes follow and he sees the knife in its scabbard. Clay walks away to join the others on the trail, and after a moment, Bennie follows.

Now, Bennie still lies on the gritty stone, facing the sun, his thoughts audible: "All I see is a deep fiery red, like a furnace blasting me, burning me in flames of hell..."

Clay's voice breaks in: "Okay, Bennie... fire building." In another flashback, Clay is again standing over Bennie. He kneels next to where Bennie sits, and Bennie moves away.

"First," Clay says, "flint and steel." Bennie's eyes follow as Clay takes his knife from its sheath. Clay repeatedly hits the thick edge of the blade against a piece of flint. "See, I'm striking the sparks into your tinder..." Without a word, Bennie stands up and walks away. Clay stops what he's doing and watches him go, then replaces the knife on his belt.

Back on his stone bed under the blazing sun, Bennie's thoughts continue: "You're doing well, sun, fry me like an egg, sizzling on the griddle... bake me on this hot sandstone, tall and strong... sandstone is nothing but little grains of sand... " His left fingertips run gently across the fine grit surface.

"Come on, you buzzards with your long red necks, crooked beaks, evil eyes, come tear my flesh, pick at my heart... oh, don't be afraid of this knife in my hand. I would never use it on *you*. These six inches of hot steel... steel... steel." With each utterance of the word, we see his theft repeated, his hand stealthily lifting the knife from its sheath, then again, closer, then again, even closer.

"...Little grains of sand..." His eyes stay closed against the fierce sun. The sweat on his forehead is sucked away by the dry air. Now he's remembering again...

Another boy on the expedition, Will, has spilled his bag of trail mix. He's on his knees trying to pick the pieces out of the sand. He looks up to see Bennie handing him his own bag of food. Will takes it with gratitude, then Bennie helps him to his feet. They don't realize that Clay is watching this exchange.

Bennie's closed eyelids twitch in the harsh light. His thoughts are jumbled. "...Grains of sand, all sticking together..." His fist holding the knife trembles. "...six inches of hot...steel..." Again, he sees his own fingers steal the knife. "...in my heart..." The knife in his fist trembles more. "...blood-red sandstone tall as the sky, and hard and strong and... bloody..."

His right hand suddenly brings the knifepoint to his chest, stopping just at his t-shirt, inches from his heart. His left hand joins it there, poised to plunge in the blade.

"...grains of sand... sticking together..." Bennie's eyes pop open. He remembers his hand giving food to Will, and again, a closer image of the same, and again, closer, his own hand giving.

Eyes wide, he remembers Clay's voice: "I saw you give your food to Will, Bennie. I know that's a hard thing to do, and I appreciate it. I respect you for it."

The gleaming knifepoint hovers at his chest as Clay goes on: "That's the only way we'll make it through this... if we're like this sandstone. You know, it's nothing but a billion little grains of sand, all sticking together... but these ol' walls are pretty darn tall and strong; seems like they last forever."

Bennie's eyes, staring up at the sun, are beginning to water. He blinks tears away. He remembers handing his food to Will, and hears Clay say again, "...and I appreciate it. I respect you for it...."

Bennie's hands lift the knife from his chest and drop it clattering on the stone, as Clay's voice continues, "So if you need me and it's really important, you blow that whistle."

Bennie leaps to his feet, jumps off the boulder, and runs, runs back the way he came, searching until he finds it: the whistle. He drops to his knees, shakes sand out of the whistle, brings it to his lips, and blows.

The long, shrill note of the whistle echoes in the empty canyons.

We see Clay kneeling under a gnarled tree, taking the empty scabbard off his belt. He hears the whistle, stands, re-fastens his belt, and strides toward the sound, out of frame. The stark landscape image holds, then dissolves.

Now, the desert in morning light, both cruel and beautiful, seems empty as we hear Clay: "Alright you guys, this is the last canyon. We're almost home!"

A chorus: "Woo-hoo! Yip, yip, yippee!"

The group of guys enters the frame, walking away, and we see Clay's belt with the knife in its scabbard. As they trudge down the trail, Clay puts an arm around Bennie's shoulder. They laugh and keep on walking, on past the cliffs and boulders of sandstone.

Credits roll and music swells. The End.

*

My little imaginary movie, the sweet, unrealized creation of my naive twenty-year-old self, faded to black in the blackness of my dungeon, in the prison of my jaded forty-year-old self. Sentimental tears were on my cheeks, but I didn't care. It had taught me something about who I am, if I am anything at all.

This son of atheist commies had crafted a metaphor for prayer, forgiveness, redemption.

Yes, yes! I said to myself. *It seems I am a man of faith and have always been so, despite every protestation of agnosticism, every cynical disillusionment. An idealist I was, and so I remain: a believer in the good, in the power of unity, in the force of love. I always knew, long before Lester Spanda preached it to me, that all we pathetic and noble humans, and all the things in this beautiful and terrible world, are not separate.*

"We are One," I whispered aloud into the darkness. And

the Observer said: *Just look at yourself. Without a doubt, you have lost your mind.*

22: UNION

Darkness. Cheek on cold concrete. Spanda nowhere near but voice echoing: "Ben! Maharaj told us—'There is no need of a way out! Don't you see that a way out is also a part of the dream? All you have to do is to see the dream as dream.'"

Cate and Ava, a movie I once saw. Long ago. Movies are dreams.

Cate and Ava, a movie that I failed to finish. I tried to make it but lost my way. Forgot how, in a dream. My most important work, all ashes in my hands.

I betrayed them, failure that I am. Now they are ripped from me. My body has two bleeding wounds, one adult-size under the right arm, the other child-size under the left.

I may die of this.

Instead, I sleep. My hip and shoulder hurt. I struggle up to consciousness, breathe and stretch and meditate as I have learned. I sleep and dream.

Inside my chest is a wide open sky at dusk filled with a murmuration of cliff swallows, thousands in synchronous flow, rippling across the liquid blue in huge sweeps, folds, up-twisting arabesques, and a sound like rushing waters, far then near then far.

Time. No hours or minutes or seconds, just time, a boundless solid. Then nothing but darkness and sometimes his voice. He speaks kindly, so much repetition. "You are not in the world," he says. "The world is in you." Then silence.

*

Blind, I grasp for images. Image, as in imagination. Or is it memory? A photo album. Pictures of myself as an infant. There is one, black and white, in which I am in the arms of my smiling young father, and I gaze wide-eyed at the camera. Now, in my black cell, I imagine holding that little baby, my own beginning self, looking into his eyes, making a connection. I invite him to join me, and as I hug him to my chest, I feel a burst of warmth as he dissolves into me. Then I recall another, in which I must have been three, squinting in sunshine, wearing a New York Yankees outfit with cap and tiny glove. I do the same, making eye contact, inviting him to join me, hugging that little me with love until he vanishes into my chest.

I don't know how long I spend doing this, but I work my way up through every stage of my life—rowdy young boy, insecure teen, earnest young adult, busy grown man, husband and father—acknowledging each earlier me, bringing him with love into the me of today.

Then I go further. I imagine myself in the future: aged fifty, sixty, seventy, eighty, a very old man, body bowed but healthy... each time looking this imagined self in the eyes and hugging him into light and air inside my chest. Then I see myself on my deathbed, wrinkled and frail, eyes closed, an ancient being breathing his final breaths. I visualize gathering this rickety assemblage of skin and bones into my arms, absorbing my own dying self in a wave of pure acceptance.

And then I go further yet. I imagine my dead body, the face a still mask, the flesh inert as a log, buried in earth, eaten by worms, rotting, breaking down, crumbling into unrecognizability, becoming soil. And I see this: as it... he... I... disappears forever, the Witness still remains.

*

Now I am moving through a desert, but it is not a real

desert. It is a movie, but the cinematographer has overexposed the film. Everything is burnt out to vivid white, no shadows. Cliffs and spires, insubstantial as light through clear celluloid, tower into a blazing white sky. The soundtrack is not silence, it is the absence, or perhaps presence, of all sound. Walls merge into skyscrapers, a city-canyon, snow-bleached, blinding glare on glass. There is no sun; the sun is everywhere, but without heat or dryness. The ground is air. I have no feet. I am only eyes, squinting against the brightness as I travel. Everything is in slow motion, an infinitely varied landscape-cityscape unfolding in oceans of brilliance, ever-changing, ever the same. After a time that is long and short, I understand that in fact, I am not eyes. Eyes cannot see themselves. The witness and the witnessed are one. There can be no "I" that is separate from this desert, this city, this motion, this light. There is only current experience, all-enveloping. There is only what is, arising in awareness.

23: CONFRONTATION

Time is irrelevant but there is a perception of the alternating sequence of night and day. They make themselves known by Spanda's silence or sound, and by the quality of light filtering through the hole in this wall... or is it the hole in this skull?

A night came when this mind was awake and listening to the symphony of silence in its little universe. Spanda seemed to be sleeping. I—can I truthfully say "I"?—observed with benign curiosity as awareness shifted to each fluctuation in the tone and rhythm of this body's breath, coursing blood, churning organs, the subtle vibrations of the concrete walls, the floor and the earth beneath, plus the tiny rustles that came through the hole, the hole that was an ear—my ear?—to the outer world. If such a thing exists.

The ambient surf of nightsound was pierced by mechanical clicks and a creak I knew to be the door of Spanda's room. Someone had entered. My eyes opened and I saw light stream through the hole: the yellow glow of what I had learned was Spanda's bedside lamp. The sound of his bed creaking, then his voice:

"So, it's you at last."

Another voice, a man, flat and curt: "Where's Rose?"

"Ha, isn't that your department?"

"I know he's been here. I want you both at the same time."

I moved as soundlessly as possible, craning my neck to see something through the hole. No luck.

"I'm just a simple church caretaker, my friend. Do as you will."

"Dunne, you've always been a fool."

Then I heard the unmistakable spit of a pistol with a silencer. Just like in the movies. Immediately there were the multiple thuds of a body, knees-arms-torso-head, crumpling to the floor.

Long silence, then the rustling of clothing, footsteps, thumps, objects moved, and eventually something heavy being dragged across the floor. The light clicked off and I heard the door open, more dragging, the door close. Silence, darkness, time... then light on, water noise, dry swishes, sweeping. A door. Silence and darkness again, seeming without end, as if it had all been a dream.

I woke up some unknown time later. The dim bluish light that I presumed was daylight from a curtained window streamed through the hole, but I heard only the busier, more external sort of silence that was common to the daytime hours.

I was hungry. It was probably breakfast time, but none was offered. I meditated, I stretched, I meditated again. Thoughts passed with emptiness between. Untold hours went by. Spanda was gone. Spanda was dead. What else could it be? And the murderer was looking for me.

Maybe it was the weakness that came with hunger and thirst, maybe it was just the urge to escape, but I found myself slipping into sleep again, a restless, uncomfortable sleep that came and went and came again until I was entirely disoriented. I guessed that another day and night had passed; it seemed to be morning but I couldn't be sure. I used the bucket, but it was now smelling foul.

Then I heard a knock at the door, Spanda's door. My heart jumped: rescue! But immediately I remembered the cruel voice: *Where's Rose?* I sat silently. The knock came again, then after a moment the lock clicked and the door creaked open. I heard a footstep or two but nothing else. I imagined eyes looking around the room. My heart was thumping. I wanted to yell out, but I wanted to stay alive. After a moment, whoever it was went out the door and closed it behind them.

I sat with my head hung down in the darkness. I was numb, caught between relief and regret. Had fear ruled me, or was it good sense? I observed how easy it had been for me to slip back into identification with this body, this personality, this illusory self built on fictions. I had journeyed far beyond, but the threat of physical injury or death pulled me right back to earth. I had so much yet to learn.

Now I sat and remembered holding in my arms the tiny body of my newborn daughter, then her bigger body as I rocked her to sleep after a nightmare in her second year. So many such nights. Tears still on her soft cheek, her little mouth open in utter surrender to sleep at last, warmth and the scent of baby powder seeping through her pajamas. I remembered the sweetest moments between Cate and I, locking eyes across the sleeping child between us, knowing that we were perfect, a family, forever.

I once again ran my fingers around the edges of the little door in the wall. After all these days without eyesight, my fingertips had become like eyes. They could easily tell the wood surface of the door from the rougher concrete around it. I found the hinges, then explored the fine crack on the opposite side, moving inch by inch until I found a tiny indentation. I tried my index fingernail, middle fingernail, thumbnail, middle finger again, prying with all the meager leverage I could get, until I broke the nail. I swore and curled the finger inside my tight fist until the pain subsided. The door hadn't budged.

I took off my belt. The little prong of metal on the buckle was the smallest and strongest tool I had. My fingers found the indentation again in the darkness and with both hands I worked the prong into it, digging and digging, prying, until I began to feel some crumbling of cement, some chipping of wood. I worked it up and down, back and forth, pushing deeper, then prying back. The door moved toward me a sixteenth of an inch. I kept going. My hands were feeling cramped but I kept pushing and digging until I had a good half inch leverage. I pushed the prong into the wood as hard as I could and pried one more time. The door popped open.

This inner door was a slab of hardwood two inches thick. Beyond it was a black space almost as deep as the length of my arm, and another small door whose shape was etched by a thin line of light. There had to be some kind of lock on the other side, perhaps a padlock, maybe a sliding bolt. I knew I'd have to kick it with all my strength, over and over again, to rip the screws out of the wall. First I decided to test it. Lying flat on the floor, I reached my right arm in and gave the door a shove. With almost no resistance at all, it swung open.

My body went limp with a sudden, unbearable realization. I just lay there on the floor, facing this knowledge: I had never really been a prisoner at all. I was treated like a prisoner, so I behaved like a prisoner. I had had many opportunities to escape exactly as I just did.

I was my own jailer. A victim of no one but myself. Until this moment, such had been my life. No more.

24: FREEDOM

I scrambled through the door and crawled out from under a table draped with a long fringed skirt that disguised the secret door. I was in Spanda's one-room apartment. The illumination in the room was low, but still it hurt my eyes. I squinted and looked around me. A metal-framed single bed next to a small cabinet of drawers, a counter with a miniature sink and a toaster oven, a few shelves with rows of cans and boxes of food, a mini-fridge below. A mirror and a photo of an elderly man on the wall. There was no phone or clock in the room. A door to a tiny bathroom stood wide open. Daylight came in through a high narrow window that I saw now was not covered with a curtain but by a thick tangle of tall shrubs outside.

Now what? As much as I craved fresh air and sunshine, I stopped myself from fleeing like a bird from a cage. Was Spanda's killer out there, ready to ambush me? I at least had to wait for the cover of darkness. The light was dim but it wasn't safe to turn on the room lights. I didn't know how many hours of daylight were left. I looked around me. Spanda's bed was rumpled, but I could see no sign of the violence I had heard. Nothing overturned, no blood on the floor.

The room felt sad and empty. As angry as I had been at Spanda, right now I wished he was not dead. Apparently, he had been right: the dungeon had kept me alive. So far.

The first thing I did was drink a large glass full of water, then another. I grabbed an apple from the counter and ate it as I looked around the room. Where was my stuff?

I looked under the bed and there, pushed to the back against the wall, were my sandals, my notebook and pen, and my camcorder case. Inside the case I found my wallet with all its contents intact, but no camera. There was also a stack of tapes, maybe a dozen, which made no sense. I remembered bringing only the one in the camera plus an extra. Why had Spanda bought tapes? He had recorded himself telling his story to me, but what else? The tapes had scribbles on the labels: dates and times that had been crossed out and replaced by new dates and times, several times each. Were these surveillance tapes, being re-recorded over?

I took a fresh look around the room, and there it was. A glint of glass peeked out between two cans on a shelf. He had put the camera there, facing the room, to record whatever was happening. Luckily the killer hadn't found it. I picked up the camera and carefully lifted the power cord from behind several cans and boxes, where it snaked invisibly across the shelf and down to the power outlet next to the toaster oven. From the camera, I took off a little piece of duct tape he had apparently used to cover the red light that indicated Record mode. The light was off now because the tape had reached its end, probably sometime after Spanda's murder.

Brilliant—he had plotted to capture his own killer!

I opened the fold-out screen, pushed the Rewind button for a few seconds, then hit Play. I saw a dim and grainy image of part of the empty room, but it was even more lifeless than a still photo. The only motion was the digital readout in the lower right of the picture, rolling through the numerals as seconds passed, then a minute. Good, he had thought to set up the time stamp.

I felt paranoid; I wanted to settle in and watch this tape, find the crucial scene, but I was too nervous. It would have to wait. I clicked off the playback and when the picture switched to a live image, it showed me the current time and date: 08/03/95 – 16:43:11 and counting. Almost 5 p.m., fourteen days from the day I first entered this church.

Two full weeks gone from my life, never to return. What did this mean? What had changed?

In the bathroom I was accosted by a mirror over the tiny sink. "You look like shit," I heard myself mutter. Pale face, sunken eyes with a wild stare, goatee gone shaggy to blend with the growth covering cheeks and jaw. A stranger.

I didn't know what the world out there had in store for me, but I knew this: I was a different man from the one I'd been when I walked in here. Maybe not better or worse, just different. Everything in the world has both sides built in, both dark and light. This too.

I had an ache, a physical pain in my chest and arms, an ache to hold Cate and Ava, to hug them tight. But my life was in danger from a psycho killer. To go home would put them in danger too; it would be a betrayal. Was there a way to let Cate know I was alive without putting her at risk? It required pondering and planning but I needed action, movement.

First, I had to remove the traces of my captivity to keep my pursuer in the dark. I crawled back into my dungeon and got the stinking bucket. I dumped it in the toilet, cleaned the bucket in the shower, and left it under the skirted table. I retrieved my belt, and shoved the foam pad and pillow that had been my floor for the last two weeks under Spanda's bed. I said a goodbye that was not entirely hateful, and closed the inner and outer doors to the cell.

In the dungeon I must have gotten accustomed to my own smell, but now it slowly came to my awareness that I stank. I seriously wanted to take a shower, but again, I didn't dare let my guard down like that. I settled for quickly getting naked, splashing myself at the kitchen sink, then changing into a pair of Spanda's boxers and one of his T-shirts, dark blue. I wore my shorts and sandals but my underwear and shirt went into a plastic bag destined for the first dumpster I saw.

Next I packed up the camera and all the tapes, slid the notebook into an outer pocket of the case, put my wallet in my pocket, and searched the entire apartment for my car keys. I found my wristwatch on Spanda's dresser, its battery apparently dead, but no keys anywhere. I devoured a Snickers bar as I scoured the counters and the mini-fridge for other snacks I could stuff in a bag to take with me. All this time it felt like a clock was ticking, like someone was coming to kill me so I had to run. But to run before dark would surely get me killed as well.

My fear of the assassin was so consuming that it never occurred to me that I could be considered a suspect in Spanda's murder. Maybe I was unwittingly leaving clues everywhere, a trail for the cops. I didn't wipe the place for fingerprints, but it was a good thing that I did my hurried best to leave the place clean—as if I had never been there, never even existed.

Finally I couldn't take it any longer. The summer night had not yet fallen but twilight was underway and the room was becoming too murky to do anything. I slung my camera bag across my chest, grabbed my bags of food and dirty clothes, and slowly, carefully turned the knob, not knowing what I would encounter. The apartment door opened into a dark passageway lit only by daylight through the transom over another door. To my left was darkness that I guessed led to a boiler room. I silently clicked the door closed behind me, turned right and tiptoed to the outer door, where I did it again: turned the knob and pushed the door open in cautious slow motion. I poked my head out and, for the first time in two weeks, breathed blessed open air.

The evening was lovely, the summer air sweet, the temperature perfect, with everything awash in the faintest golden light, the last moments of sunset. My poor eyes were blinking like crazy, but I couldn't hold back a smile, danger or no. What a beautiful world!

The door had opened under an iron-grate landing where apparently there was a rear door to a higher floor. To my left and overhead was the underside of a metal staircase trimmed in baroque wrought iron. It seemed this was the rear of the church. I was looking out at a wide lawn toward the dead end of a street, across which was a delightfully dark and tangled stand of trees. That was my destination. I slipped out and stood against the closed door in the shadow of the staircase, waiting for my moment. When the light slid from gold to gray, I clutched my bags and, like the homeless man that I was, scurried for shelter.

I must have been a comical sight as I thrashed about in the bushes, in a hurry to hide. But no one was around and I soon made it in amongst bigger trees that cut out the light of the sky. I climbed a steep little bluff and scrambled over boulders in the growing darkness, until I found a spot at the base of a big trunk, screened from the view of the roads on either side.

I sat down, settled in, listened carefully for any sound of pursuit, then took a deep breath. For now, I felt safe. Safe in the dark. I fumbled through the food bag, my eyes blind again but my fingertips smart, until I found some carrot sticks, and munched while I thought about my predicament. I couldn't rely on finding my car; clearly Spanda had taken it someplace where it couldn't betray my presence. I couldn't contact Cate, in case whoever wanted me dead was watching her or had tapped our phones. Still, it didn't take long to make a plan.

First, I sat for an unknowable duration, waiting for the hums and flickers of cars passing on the nearby street to decline in frequency. Sitting in darkness, I scanned with slow care my memory of this neighborhood, conjuring images from my first and second visits over two weeks ago.

The streets began to quiet; it was getting late but I knew the prudent thing would be to wait even later. I couldn't do it. I crept out of the bushes and hurried along the closest road. As I expected, it was Delaware Avenue. Within three blocks I saw it: the O'Brien home. In the moonlight I could make out a For Sale sign on the front lawn.

As a car passed, I froze and shrunk into the blackness under the trees. Then, like a rat in a dark alley, I scuttled through shadows to the back of the house. I jiggled an old double-hung window until it creaked open bit by bit, and I was inside. My assumption was correct that the house was empty, but I crept with exaggerated care, silent, step by step through dark rooms. Everything seemed as it had been, except that the flowers were gone and the air smelled stale. I found the phone in the same location and was immensely grateful that it had a dial tone. In my bag was Auster's card but I didn't dare turn on a light. I found a bathroom, took several slow minutes covering the window with a towel, and then turned on the light just long enough to memorize the number. Then it was back out to the phone, again feeling my way in the gloom.

Auster answered on the third ring.

IN THE NOT-KNOWING

25: CABIN

I had followed my gut, never an easy task for me, and gambled that Auster was on my side. Thankfully, I was right. But I couldn't yet know how much of a friend he really was.

His voice was gruff on the phone: "It's late; who is this?"

In a whisper I blurted half-incoherent apologies for the lateness of the call and for getting him involved in my drama, even though he may not remember who I am, and I begged him to help me but to tell no one. I babbled until he cut me off.

"Ben Rose? Thank goodness!"

"What do you mean?" I was surprised by the genuine relief in his voice.

"You're alive! People are looking for you; your wife of course, the police, me. And I thought something very bad had—"

"Bad, yes! I'm in danger and so is everyone who—"

"Don't say any more. Where are you?"

The fact that I was calling from the O'Brien home seemed to be meaningful to him, to cement his action plan. In less than an hour, he had picked me up in his car and we were on our way out of Kingston, heading west into the Catskills. I must have fed him a jumbled tale; I don't remember. I fought sleep but my eyes would not stay open on that ride; my memory is only fractured glimpses, narrow dark roads curving in headlights.

I woke up when we reached our destination: a rustic little structure that sat on a low rise fifty yards up a rutted

driveway from the paved road, in a moonlit clearing surrounded by dense black forest. Paul told me it belonged to
his photographer friend, who would return in the fall. We
were on Woodland Valley Road, he said, near a village called
Phoenicia. I took a deep breath of cool mountain air. The
stars were brilliant. As it turned out, this well-stocked, cozy
cabin in a quiet, beautiful setting was to be my home for
more than a month as I began to reassemble my life. So
much better than a dark concrete cell.

Auster listened as I paced the tiny, shadowy living room
telling the story again, more coherently this time. I was des-
perate to keep my wife and daughter safe from the murderous people I was entangled with, so I convinced Paul, against
his initial impulse, to hold off on telling Cate where I was,
or even that I was alive. He left and I was alone with my
thoughts in the wee hours, grasping for the diamond inside,
holding to the calm witness, watching without judgment as
a creeping fog of failure and despair arose in the emotional
field of this self called Ben Rose, arose, lingered a moment,
then passed like a cloud in the sky. Gone.

After a couple more hours of exhausted sleep—aah, a real
bed, with sheets and a pillow!—then a cup of delicious coffee outside in the fresh, pine-scented morning, I was beginning to return to a sense of normalcy. My curiosity had
been burning; I pulled out my camera and the stack of tapes.
Hunched over the cafe-size table in the cabin's narrow
kitchen, I searched backwards on the latest tape until I saw
murky images of something happening. Unfortunately,
Spanda had not aimed the hidden camera in the perfect
direction to cover the room, and the lighting was dim. But
there he was: the intruder. I was stunned to recognize an
odd quick gesture I'd seen before, hand to forehead, and the
expressionless profile in grainy half-silhouette: Nils Nilsson. So he was not merely a liar, but a killer as well.

I played the footage several times, watching and listening

as closely as I could on the little screen. Just Nilsson's head and shoulders were visible in the lower left of the frame, and for only a few seconds. Spanda, judging from Nilsson's eye direction, must have been sitting on his bed, out of sight of the camera. They exchanged a few words just as I remembered, all of it faint but audible, then Nilsson was gone from the image. A second later came the report of the pistol, the sound of Spanda's body hitting the floor, then the long series of clean-up noises. Twice it seemed that Nilsson crossed in front of the lens but it was just a passing black blur; otherwise the camera frame was empty.

Whoever had come into the room many hours later, not long before I escaped, was nowhere to be seen. I assumed the tape had come to an end before that point. The other tapes with numerous dates on the labels showed nothing but the same dim shot of an empty room.

Then I saw a tape labelled in Spanda's blocky print: "Les Talking." It contained his entire confession of the Yasser Arafat episode and his life afterward, exactly as I remembered him telling me as I crouched in my dark cell. The audio quality was reasonably good, but as I should have expected, he had taken care not to include his face in the picture. The image showed him from approximately chest to knees, seated, his hands occasionally gesturing, his legs crossing and uncrossing once. Not the image I wanted, but the story was all there in sound. A plan began to form in my mind.

Late in the afternoon, Auster showed up to bring me some clothes and supplies, and to discuss our next steps. I showed him the video of Spanda's confession, then the clip of Nilsson just before the shooting.

"Wait. Let me see that again," he said, leaning in to peer closely at the screen. I played it twice more for him. I told him that this was the guy I had mentioned before, who had given me a fake business card and recommended I visit the church where I ended up a prisoner.

"I would swear," he said at last, "that that is a guy I know as someone entirely different. An investment counselor from California, he said. But I had my suspicions."

"Nils Nilsson," I said.

"I know him as Noel Nachtmann," Auster said. "Isn't that great, an alliterating assassin."

"Ha ha, not funny."

"There's more about him in those papers I put on the table. Read them after I leave."

"What the hell am I mixed up in?"

"It's like some kind of game, but a serious one. He said he wanted you too."

"Right. But I can't just hide forever, and stay away from my family. I've been thinking a lot and I have an idea.... This guy counts on his anonymity, right?"

"Yeah, his invisibility."

"What if we let it be known publicly that we know who he is, we have video and a name. Two names. He'd be blocked."

"Hmm, I don't know. That's either completely crazy, or just crazy enough to work."

We went on talking into the evening hours over beers and grilled burgers. We sketched out a convoluted strategy that we called "Lester's Movie." Between his police and media connections and my video editing abilities, Paul and I would set events in motion that would build an invisible shield against this murderous bastard, Nilsson or Nachtmann or ... ?

26: PLOT

As I look back on those days from all these years later, our defensive plan, our preemptive strike, seems both foolish and, in a sense, inconsequential. It's impossible to know if all our busy effort had any effect at all. It seemed vital at the time, but perhaps it was mostly just a way for me to occupy my mind, to feel less like a prisoner cowering in fear. We launched our campaign and the steps rolled out in order:

1. Paul had already told me all about the burned body in my car and the police investigation. Now, he let his detective friend know that not only was I alive, but that I had video evidence of a murder that might be linked to that incineration. And I was hiding from a killer.

2. Detective Peluso came with Paul to the cabin and looked at the footage. He kept a poker face, but I could tell he felt the video was important. I was sure of that when he told us that the pastor of the Ponckhockie Union Congregational Church had reported his caretaker, Lester Spanda, as missing.

3. Peluso acknowledged that my family would be endangered by my presence, so he contacted Cate without letting her know the full truth. He presented it like this: it was a missing person case (no mention of homicide or a burned car) and there was substantial reason to suspect that I, also a missing person, had been involved. But at this time he was not allowed to tell her what the reason was.

4. As part of his investigation, Peluso got a warrant to remove my video-editing computer and its peripherals from the Jersey City office, on the pretext that it might contain communications or other information linked to the case. I was as grateful for his willingness to stretch the truth as I was for his networking skill with law enforcement agencies outside his jurisdiction. The equipment was removed by Jersey City police in Peluso's presence, and he subsequently brought it to me. My intention was to edit the footage shot by Lester Spanda.

5. With the help of Auster, who procured still images for me from local libraries, I put together a rough mini-documentary. The little kitchen table was my workstation. I used the "Les Talking" footage as the narration, the A roll. As B roll, I overlaid images and newspaper clippings of Arafat, Cairo, the PLO, Black September, assassination attempts, IDF, Mossad, Bombay slums, Nisargadatta Maharaj, New York City, and of course, the Ponckhockie Union Congregational Church. I snipped out the identifying references to me, and much of the Indian non-dualist philosophizing. I bookended Spanda's story with my own voice, electronically disguised, testifying that he had told this story directly to me but that I must remain anonymous for my own safety. I also stated that in addition to the recording of him, there was also hidden-camera footage of everything that occurred in his apartment for two weeks, including visitors. "The footage is currently being examined by police for clues to the caretaker's subsequent disappearance," I announced.

6. Meanwhile, Auster had been using all his journalist resources to research Spanda's story about the

assassination and impersonation. As we expected, he found nothing to support it.

7. Next, Auster released copies of my edited tape to local media outlets, using his relationships to stir up attention to the outrageous claim that Yasser Arafat had been replaced by an impostor. At first he treated it as potentially credible, a real scoop. Then he began to use the phrase "conspiracy theory" and dropped hints that Spanda was some sort of vagrant crackpot who worked as a church janitor, nothing more.

8. Research by others also failed to turn up any evidence. But even before that, Lester's Movie was already making its way to regional and then national news outlets, with headlines like "Church Caretaker Claims To Be Arafat Assassin." More than once the pastor was interviewed and he described his employee as friendly but secretive, efficient but eccentric. He mentioned entering Spanda's apartment under the church after he'd been missing a couple of days, but finding nothing. Then I knew—that's who I had heard when I'd been too afraid to call out.

9. No sooner had Lester's claim spread wide, than it began to be loudly debunked. Calmer minds prevailed over hysterical speculation; after all, there was no corroborating evidence. The PLO issued a flat rejection of the story as "irresponsible fabrication." Reputable sources stated that clearly this whole thing was a nasty hoax or a pathetic delusion, perpetrated by bad people who were now afraid to come forward. Not missing, just hiding.

10. So I had what I wanted. First, Nilsson's shadowy bosses would not feel permanently threatened because the discrediting of Spanda was the best

possible technique to keep their secret safe, to hide it in plain sight. Assuming they existed at all, we had given them a lovely gift. At the same time, Nilsson (whom we had started to call NN, or Double Naught) would suspect that we had footage of him killing Spanda, so he would not dare expose himself further by coming after me or my family.

That was it—ten steps like the plot of a TV movie. You construct it according to the formula; it has its desired effect. This part of the story was one hundred percent consuming to me for those few weeks—life and death, in fact—but looking back on it from all these years later, I find it the least important chapter. Like so many plots without enough deep mystery, ultimately forgettable.

27: CHANGE

We had strategized and executed, and after the month it took for it all to play out, I deemed it successful. There were no guarantees, of course. NN may still be gunning for me, but he hadn't arrived yet. As the days and weeks went by, my anxiety about him began to fade. I saw it like this: NN was Death. All of us live with the knowledge of our eventual demise; it's a fact of human life. To live in fear of death is to surrender one's own power. I decided I would work towards health and be vigilant against accidents, and I would carry on with my life in acceptance and gratitude. I had done what I could. NN would have no power over me.

So, as far as such things can be determined, the plan had accomplished its goal. Nevertheless, I felt as far away from celebration as one can feel, for two reasons:

First, I was nagged by a sad feeling about Spanda. He had inflicted something terrible on me, put me through hell in fact, but I couldn't deny that he also may have saved my life. I did not hate him, and I didn't like to think about his burning corpse.

Second and much the bigger of the two… after Detective Peluso met Cate, he reported this to me: Cate was in the process of moving both home and office. I was bewildered. Where could she be going, and why? He persuaded her to reveal that she and Ava were moving into her parents' home. He said her demeanor was of one in mourning, as if she thought I was dead and it was time for her to move on. It hurt me to hear this. I wanted so badly to let Cate and Ava know I was alive and would be with them soon. But then I thought, just a few more days, a few more days until I can begin to feel safe enough for a reunion. Then, once we've reconnected, time will pass and wounds will heal.

And then I found the audio recording. This would have been probably about August 15th. After the flurry of activity setting up my editing station, gathering material, editing Lester's Movie and putting it into the world, there was finally a slow moment. That's when I noticed that there on the computer desktop among the program icons, not hidden in any project folder, was the sound file labeled "To Ben."

I listened until the recording ended, sunken in the swamp of Cate's voice. When I could rouse myself from wounded stupor, I saw that the date on the file was August 3rd. She had recorded it the day I escaped, nearly two weeks ago.

Nate Nixon. Of course. The alliterating assassin strikes again. NN, Double Naught, double knot like a noose, Death himself. He had been hovering over her even before he descended on me. I had never protected her at all. And unwittingly, she had sent the predator to his prey: both victims in one swoop. Or so NN had hoped, as he laughed at her gullibility. Poor Spanda. Grateful me. Deluded Cate.

I had to do something. Safety be damned, I called Cate from the cabin. No answer at either our apartment or office phones. When I called her parents' home, her mother answered. I did not want to reveal anything to her, so I disguised my voice and asked for Ms Cate Cross, regarding a business matter. After a moment, she answered.

I'm not sure why, but my voice was almost a whisper: "Cate, it's Ben."

I heard an intake of breath, nothing more.

"Cate... I'm okay. I'm hiding from people who want to hurt us. I'm so sorry I couldn't talk to you until now."

More silence, then: "Where are you?"

"I can't tell you, it's not safe."

"Ben, what the fuck have you done?" There was a hard edge in her voice that gave way to a trembling moan by the end of her question.

"I'll tell you all about it later. I have to get off the phone, but I needed to tell you I'm okay and we'll be together soon." Too little, too late, I feared.

"No, we won't." The steely edge had returned to her voice.

"What do you mean?"

"Somehow, I knew this all along, that you were alive, hiding somewhere, running away from us. So now it's confirmed. We're done, Ben. We're fucking done."

The phone clicked dead in my ear. I re-dialed.

She answered with a shout of rage: "Don't call me!"

"I want to see Ava!" I yelled, but she had hung up again.

I sat for a long time with my head in my hands. Bruce Cockburn's song, "What About the Bond?" rose up in me, an angry protest. *Goddamnit, didn't we have some sort of mystical unity? You want to throw it all away?*

Maybe time would heal this. Maybe she would soften. Maybe I could fix the damage with an outpouring of love, once we were all back together again. Maybe....

But everything was different now. After all that had happened, the end of my family was still the most profound change I had yet faced.

Who am I if not a family man? Every other way that I had ever defined myself was fading away to a faint echo in the reverberating silence of the dark space I had traversed. But would I have to let go of this one as well? The dream of a perfect family was embedded in me deep, deeper than I had realized. Husband + Father = Man. Right? If I am neither, do I even exist at all?

As the ensuing weeks unfurled, my attachment to that

simplistic formula had to be abandoned. My family was no longer. It seemed impossible, yet it was true.

28: CAMP

After the intense focus of editing Lester's Movie was over and it was making its way into the world, my days at the cabin were empty.

One morning as I looked in the mirror I was suddenly disoriented by the shaggy creature staring back at me. Auster had brought me shaving supplies but I hadn't bothered to use them. On an impulse I grabbed scissors, shaving cream, razor, and went to work. I didn't stop until both scalp and face were smooth and hairless. The naked countenance in the mirror now was no less a stranger, but I was glad it was different.

I sent postcards to my mother and sister, letting them know I was okay. I asked Auster to mail them on one of his jaunts into Dutchess County, an hour away. He also tried to call Cate on my behalf from random phone booths, but she refused to take his calls. I wrote her a letter that he mailed with no return address so neither of us could be traced—a one-way communication that only made me feel more sad and alone.

Often in the pink light of dawn I would take long walks up Woodland Valley Road or strike off up the mountainsides into untracked forest. I was fascinated by the long straight rows of piled stones that ran uphill and down through empty woods, apparently the tumbled remains of walls made by pioneer farmers attempting to subsist in a frontier wilderness, possibly dating to Revolutionary times or even earlier.

Other days I walked down the narrow valley until it opened up wider to the sky and I could see more houses here and there on the forested slopes. That's when I turned around and went back. I always stopped short of entering the village of Phoenicia, still cautious, still holding to the safety of invisibility.

Trapped in the cabin one rainy morning, I finally turned my attention to what was there inside. I browsed the shelves and saw mostly books about photography. One oversized but slender volume titled "Me and My Gun: Portraits" caught my eye, and I leafed through pages of images by various photographers, including the famous posed shot of Lee Harvey Oswald holding a newspaper and a rifle. One page that I had passed with barely a glance seemed to whisper a demand for a closer look, so I turned back. The black and white image was bland and staged, an empty corner of a suburban living room in which a hearth was lined with rows of rifles and pistols, machetes were hung above the fireplace, and the floor held belts full of bullets plus a bow and arrows. In the center, looking anachronistic in a dark suit with a bowler hat and an umbrella across his knee, sat a very British-looking gentleman. The caption read, "Mercenary soldier J.D. with his weapons collection, American Fork, Utah, 1975." I leaned in closer. I could hardly accept what I was seeing, but without a doubt, it was Jack Dunne: Lester Spanda.

Like so many other things I had experienced that summer, it did not seem believable that this obscure photo would be found in precisely this house, where I was hiding from the killer this crazy dead man had brought into my life. I noted the photographer's name for future reference, but I doubted I would follow up. I just wanted it all behind me, the sooner the better.

The rain disappeared early that afternoon, so I walked down Woodland Valley Road to where it curved past an empty green hillside on the right with a fence and a red structure like a small barn close to the road. This was further toward town than I had gone before. Across the street was a creek with a neighborhood of small houses on the far side. As I approached the red buildings, I was startled by a *deja vu* vibration up my spine, a chill cutting through the humid heat.

Ignoring the "Romer Mt. – Private Property" signs, I climbed the fence and walked a few yards through a grassy meadow that soon began to slope up toward dark pines. Then something stopped me. My sight seemed overlaid with a different version of the same landscape, in which I was surrounded by tall people, all facing the same direction and singing. I was small, and my left hand was up near my shoulder, enveloped by the large, strong, right hand of my father. I squinted in sunshine up at him, and he was singing too. The tune seemed sad, but he smiled as he sang. This was wondrous.

"Where have all the flowers gone?" a multitude of voices chorused in unison. When that song ended, the man with a banjo who stood on the little stage up front started another. "Guantanamera..." they all sang, and I understood none of it. But here I was with my father, just the two of us together in a crowd on a sunny summer afternoon, and everything felt utterly perfect.

It lasted only a vivid moment and I was back in my body on that muggy day in August 1995, but memories kept appearing like puzzle pieces, one after another, assembling a picture that hadn't been in my thoughts even once in over three decades. My father had taken me to check out a summer camp in the mountains that he'd been saving money for—a special camp meant for people like us, he told me. We had a wonderful day together and he promised me that I could begin attending the camp next year when I was eight. I was overjoyed, but my happiness soon curdled to sour resentment when he told me the camp had closed just a few months after our visit. I didn't understand, but I blamed him for disappointing me.

1962... yes, yes, Camp Woodland it was called. Now I was sitting on the ground by the road, leaning against the fence with my eyes closed, searching the dim vaults of memory.

"Pardon me, sir. You appear distressed. May I be of assistance?" A thin elderly man was addressing me. He had a trimmed white beard and an unruly tangle of white hair. His eyebrows were mostly black and swept up like little wings on either side. His shirt was a striking lavender.

"No, I'm fine, thank you," I said, struggling to return to the present. "But can you tell me... was there once a Camp Woodland here?"

He pointed, nodding. "The actual camp was just up that road over there, on the mountainside. A couple of buildings still stand... mostly homes there now. But the annual music events, the folk festivals every August... those took place on exactly this spot. This was the Simpson Ski Slope then." His look of concern cracked into an impish grin. "I attended many of them myself, unrepentant old socialist that I am, ha!"

"I just had such an amazing flashback," I blurted. "My father brought me here once. People were singing together."

"Probably led by Pete Seeger himself. Too bad the camp had to close down after more than twenty good years... another casualty of the idiotic Red Scare, if you ask me. Such were the times. So much more liberal today, thank the Universe, ha! And now I must continue my daily walk."

"Thank you," I said. "You've been more helpful than you know."

He strode away, but in the weeks to follow I saw him again, and in the ensuing months and years spent many treasured hours in his company. His name was Ted, a painter of carefully felt abstracts that were simultaneously geometric and sensuous, a man who would become like a second father to me, the soul-father that I had never had.

As I walked back up Woodland Valley toward the cabin, I saw on a large flat rock near the road a two-foot length of something delicately tubelike, translucent, textured. A snake had shed its old, dead skin.

29: FIRE

In front of the cabin was a room-size square of grass in the center of which was a ring of stones, a rudimentary fire pit. Many of my nights in that refuge were spent sitting by a crackling fire in solo meditation. Forever changing yet always the same, the flames worked a strange magic on me. I fell in. For hours, I stared... orange and blue flickers in a hypnotic dance, glowing golden cities of embers that grew and then crumbled. Twigs combusting in seconds, solid logs transforming by stages, everything oxidizing into light, heat, ash. Sparks ascending the column of smoke to join the stars. The non-stop bustle of sound, the snaps and sizzles. The warmth. But most of all, the flames, their liquid shapes reaching always skyward, translucent, mindless, insubstantial yet hungry, writhing and capering in infinite blazing variation, an endless river of bright motion, without pause but never dull.

Occasionally I was lulled into memories of those few nights of campfires in the desert in 1975, and it was more real than a movie. I relived the sensations, the discomfort, the insecurity, but at the same time I had a growing sensation of separation: that anxious kid was not "me."

Gazing into the flames, the simultaneous embodiment of change and not-change, I felt the fractions of time slow down and open up, and keep opening up like fractal blossoms... I began to understand how to enter a moment like a room, how to sink into the foreverness of Now. The meaning of this to the temporal me was that history has burned to the ground, that the past is oxidized into nothingness. Bygones no longer have any claim.

I am only what I am right now.

Night after night, I took this journey, a journey both opposite and parallel to the journey I had taken in a black stone cell. It was on some unknown midnight near the end of August that I observed as if from outside my body as I stood up from the fire, went into the cabin and got my digital video camera and all the tapes, brought them out and dumped them into the flames. I sat again and watched, listened, smelled. Plastic warped and bubbled, glass cracked, ribbons of tape liquified. A chemical stink arose with the smoke. There in the sun-like center of a purifying furnace, it all became an unrecognizable black mass, a volcanic cinder, a smoking meteorite. I doused the fire and went to bed.

When Auster showed up the next morning, he was horrified. I had destroyed important evidence! What was I thinking? I doubt my explanation made much sense to him, but he honored it, begrudgingly. Later, I made him feel better by reminding him that I had captured all the key footage onto my hard drive. It was not lost.

But I had changed.

30: FALL

Afterward, nothing happened.

Lester's Movie made its splash then disappeared into obscurity. There was no sign whatsoever of Nilsson/Nachtmann/Nixon. The video shots were no help in finding him, nor were the names. Eventually, months and years later, as the sense of danger faded entirely away, I toyed with the question of whether he had even existed at all. Memory is certainly not reliable. If life is a dream, then maybe NN was just a symbol, a creation of my own mind, an embodiment of my urge toward growth through challenge. He was not merely an assassin who threatened my life; he led me toward higher self-knowledge. Maybe NN was a scapegoat for a subconscious act of arson: the burning down of my life... to be followed by the building of a new one. Sometimes the killer is the savior.

The incinerated body was not identified; none of Spanda's DNA could be found, nor any fingerprints or dental records, so there was no conclusive match. Not even partial fingerprints could be obtained from the corpse; dental x-rays were taken and the remains were buried as "John Doe." It could not be proven that the burned car was mine, but mine stayed gone. Officially, the investigations continued, but they slowed down, then got slower still.

*

Nothing happened, but at the same time, a lot happened. Cate refused to speak to me. Sometimes, at night, alone,

I would descend into a gloomy analysis of my failures, a meticulous teasing apart of all my petty dysfunctions that had annoyed or disappointed her. Then the observer in me would see what I was doing, would shine a flashlight beam of awareness into the shadowy closet of gratuitous self-flagellation that I had built for myself, and it would dissolve like smoke in a breeze. Or, more often, a muscular homunculus would stand up inside my chest and shout, *Goddammit, I am not the betrayer! My name is NOT my nature!*

Cate filed for divorce and we began the difficult dance of shared custody in a hostile environment. Ava started kindergarten in a fancy suburban private school. They lived with Cate's parents. We let our Jersey City apartment and office go. I canceled my documentary proposal to SUNY and sold my computer equipment and film gear through newspaper want-ads. I rented a small apartment in Woodstock and began doing manual labor helping a local stonemason.

Paul and Siri tackled the long bureaucratic process and eventually adopted Ethan O'Brien. After several months, someone bought the O'Brien home and life there went on.

By October, exactly twenty years ago, the earthquake of that summer had subsided and the landscape, while changed, was recognizable once again.

*

Then my bad times began. Autumn in the Catskills is usually a blaze of color, postcard images everywhere you look. But in my memory, that fall was not a beautiful one. Its transition from lush summer was an abrupt browning, everything gone sere under leaden skies. I labored like a slave, eyes on the ground, and as stonework grew more scarce, I had to scrimp and deny to get by. November was a dull march, one foot in front of the other through cold rain.

I was numb, could not imagine a future. But the future came, and it was winter.

Winter, 1995-1996: a bleak landscape of isolation and struggle. I had survived the dark chamber, the deaths, the tense aftermath, the loss of my family, all as if some invisible force of sheer necessity animated my body. Now it was over. I collapsed in slow motion.

My numb twilight became dark night. I fell into a depression from which I could barely rouse myself to address the minimal requirements of living. In my little hovel attached to an old farmhouse in the woods, I shivered under a pile of smelly second-hand blankets. I ate ramen noodles, crackers, canned soup. These were my months of drunkenness and forgetting, aided by the alcoholic couple living in the main house. I despised their constant bickering but welcomed the cheap booze and potent joints they shared. Perhaps it was all inevitable, part of the script of my life, because it played out like a recapitulation, a blurry mirror image of my weeks in Spanda's dungeon. I escaped this potentially even more insidious prison with the help of two things: my friend Paul's unceasing attention, and my own deeply buried spark, my diamond of endurance, my "I am."

This period of sorry impairment is not what this story is about, but I mention it because of an interesting fact: the neighbor couple were John and Peggy. They shared the names of the two people most involved in Benedict Arnold's decline into treachery: Major John André, the British spy chief who was captured, tried, and hanged by Washington's army, and his "dear friend" Peggy Shippen Arnold, daughter of a prominent Philadelphia Loyalist, who, as Benedict's nineteen-year-old wife, became the highest paid spy in the American Revolution.

*

One midnight I sat in John and Peggy's drafty living

room, sunken in their half-collapsed couch, nursing a third glass of whiskey. Peggy was passed out and snoring on the same couch, her chubby feet on my lap. Her open mouth was half covered with tangled brown hair, her head on a throw pillow matted with cat fur. A haze hung in the room. My eyes burned. John was pacing the floor, his fleshy bulk making the boards squeak with every step. His speech was slurred.

"My book's gonna do it, man. It's gonna out-Zinn Zinn. You'll see." He stopped and took a noisy gulp from the bottle he carried. "The history we were brainwashed with in school is all fucking lies. Written by the victors, those motherfuckers. Gotta tear that house down."

"Yeah, man," I said. I felt an urge to sleep.

He abruptly walked into the next room and I heard the sounds of drawers opening and closing as he swore in a low voice. Then he strode back in, carrying a big shipping envelope stuffed full. He dropped it in my lap, on Peggy's feet.

She whined, "Hey!" Her eyes never opened. I looked in the envelope: a manuscript, hundreds of printed pages.

"There it is, what I've done so far. Read it," he commanded, scratching at a red flaky patch on his stubbled cheek. "Tell me what you think." His bossy manner, I assumed, came from his life of privilege, son of a corporate CEO: preppie private schools, country clubs. Peggy came from the same Connecticut milieu. The house that was falling apart around them had been a gift from her father. Both approaching thirty, they were trying to make their trust funds last forever, as he wrote his world-changing book on history and she explored experientially the mechanisms-of-action of various psychotropic substances.

"Now where the fuck did I put that bottle?" He walked into the adjacent room again, and I heard a breathy grunt and a creak as he sat. Then he yelled: "Go home, Ben! Go home and read!"

I did read John's book, or some of it. I gave up when I began to understand the depth of his self-deception. The man was not a writer, he was a ranter. An opinionated blowhard with mastery of neither syntax nor grammar. Maybe his research was valid and his ideas substantive, but to tease any coherent content out of the jumble of sermons and tangents was more than I could do.

He had written at some length about the American Revolution, predictably Zinn-like, emphasizing the daily lives of everyday citizens, laborers, women, the non-white, the poor. *It was a war waged by the rich upon the rich!* And so on.

Of course I sought out what he had to say about Benedict Arnold. Oddly, his focus on that episode was not through a Zinn-like socio-economic lens at all. He seemed mostly interested in espionage tricks, in codes and plots and intrigue. He explained in detail the contrivance that has come to be called the Arnold Cipher, even though it was suggested to Arnold by Major André. My namesake would write his messages to André using, in place of each word, a series of three numbers separated by periods. These numbers represented a page number of the agreed book—usually *Commentaries on the Laws of England* by William Blackstone—a line number on that page, and a word number in that line. For example, 120.9.7 would refer to the one-hundred-twentieth page, the ninth line on that page, and the seventh word in that line. In the Blackstone book, the word is "general." Without knowing the frame of reference, of course, no one could read the communication. For an extra layer of subterfuge, this numerical puzzle would be written in "invisible ink"—a mixture of ferrous sulfate and water, made visible by heat—between the lines of a friendly letter from young Peggy Arnold to her former suitor, John André.

All this cloak and dagger stuff twisted a screw in my gut. At first I didn't know why, but then I remembered the whispered stories I'd grown up with about the Rosenbergs, whose deaths haunted my parents during their early marriage, my conception, my gestation. Fear of treason and its consequences had contaminated me in the womb. What was betrayal and what was not? Who was I betraying as I huddled in stoned misery, passing a pipe with people I didn't like?

I had told John and Peggy almost nothing of my past, nor did they know my full name. They never showed any interest. I was glad I had stayed circumspect; now I could pretend that none of this historical stuff was of interest to me, so how could I have a helpful opinion about his book? Not that it mattered. Everything was forgotten in the ongoing drunken blur. Daylight always erased the night before. I returned the manuscript one morning a couple of weeks later, we chatted a bit, and that was the end of it.

The end, except for one last episode. Deep in the gloom of February, at an unknown late hour, I was again sitting on the ragged sofa as a fat joint made its way from hand to hand. John sat in his wooden rocker, gently rocking. We'd been talking about old movies and he'd just made some preposterous pronouncement that I was too stoned to refute. Peggy passed the joint to him and moved from the floor between us to sit beside me, too close.

"Benny...." She started, stopped, then continued. Her tone was sweet and plaintive. "Benny, are you lonely, hon?"

"Nah, I'm great," I said.

We sat in silence, then she said to John, "Sweetie, pass that over."

John did not respond. He took another slow hit off the joint and rocked a little harder.

She put her hand on my thigh and her head on my shoulder. I shifted an inch away but she stayed with me.

John squinted through smoke, staring stone-faced at her. His voice was flat. "Go for it, babe."

Peggy raised herself on one knee, faced me, and swung

her other knee across my legs, settling her weight on my lap. Her face was a sallow blur, my vision obscured by the cigarette-scented cowl of her long hanging hair. Then she reached into the scoop neck of her loose shirt and pulled out her breast, brushing the nipple back and forth across my lips. My body reacted immediately, the swelling in my groin pressing against her crotch. She returned the pressure, hips in a slow grind. Without my command, my hands went to her wide ass, squeezing handfuls of flesh through her sweatpants. My lips opened to take her nipple in, and she murmured, "Mmm, yes..." with ash-tray breath. I could hear John's rocker moving faster.

That's when I had a snapshot vision of the whole scene as if I were a camera mounted in a high corner of the room. A surge of energy jolted my muscles from their torpor and I stood up, tumbling Peggy to the floor with a thud that shook the walls. John never stopped rocking.

She squeaked, "What the fuck!"

"Sorry," I said. "Sorry." And I left them, slamming the door behind me.

*

Looking back on this period over the years that followed, I came to understand that my path had taken me from Spanda's dark chamber into a dark chamber of my own, a prison of my own unconscious devising. So much more difficult to see, since eyes cannot look at themselves. I sat in my depressed imaginary dungeon on the brink of self-destruction, almost forgetting forever the tiny glimpse I had had of an inexpressible cosmic unity. My experience with Spanda and NN was certainly no spiritual awakening. It was a disaster, a disaster that was also its opposite: it contained the seeds of its own reversal, a form of redemption that took much time and contemplation to blossom.

Late in March, I found a better apartment, and I never

saw John and Peggy again. I've wondered since: were those even their names? It was interesting to observe that my encounter with them seemed to transform my consuming obsession with history, to seal it off as if cauterizing a wound. My interest in the past is now merely mild, submerged under a much stronger passion for the present. At the same time, memory has become as obviously untrustworthy as television: derivative, fragmentary, faulty in its origination, heavily edited, and full of obscure personal symbols. Perhaps no more than a dream.

31: MILLENNIUM

The intervening years have been full. The world provides drama whether we want it or not. In the early nineties, on his album *The Future*, Leonard Cohen sang about how the cracks in everything let the light in. But he also sang his vision of what was to come, the now of our world, and it was bleak.

The change to a new millennium gave us the silly scare of Y2K. Not long after that came the nearly incomprehensible constitutional crisis that threatened the very foundations of our government.

President, Vice President, Speaker of the House, Cabinet members and White House officials, along with a couple of private billionaires... all brought down, indicted with thoroughly damning evidence of a false-flag plot involving explosives, planes, Islamic terrorists, and the World Trade Center. The death toll would have been horrific. An evil plan by evil men, thwarted at the last minute.

For the first time, the President Pro Tempore of the Senate advanced to the Presidency: Robert Byrd of West Virginia. He picked up the pieces of the Bush disaster, completed that term, and was re-elected for another four years. When Barack Obama was elected in 2008 and again in 2012, it was the longest run of Democratic presidents that most of us had seen in our lifetimes.

But world peace and a strong economy were still elusive. Peace can never last when war is such a profit machine. Although the capitalist warmongers could not get support for the full-scale invasion of Iraq that they claimed was necessary, Democrats and Republicans alike sponsored "police action" there, soon followed by "boots on the ground" in Afghanistan and remote-controlled drone strikes in Yemen and Pakistan. Death and destruction mounted, as oil and opium flowed. National security is always the excuse, as if there is such a thing. And members of both parties chose bailout over prosecution for the criminal bankers who created the 2008 global financial crisis. The cabals will never be eliminated.

I took interest when Yasser Arafat died in 2004, amidst some controversy about whether he had been poisoned. I wondered if he really was Bijan Zaimi... or even a second or third impersonator. If they can do it once they can do it again.

But I was glad that, whoever he was, he had been instrumental in accomplishing peace between Israel and Palestine: a two-state system that at least for now, seemed stable. If he was an impostor, was peace what his handlers wanted, or did he go rogue, and pay the price?

Are events on the world stage, as reported by the corporate showbiz media some people still call "news," actually relevant to my own small life? It's impossible to know.

*

Necessitated by child custody, Cate and I eventually returned to a cordial relationship after months of nastiness and years of frosty silence. Bit by bit, she sent back to me the things that had been mine: books, CDs and vinyl albums, videotapes, the old Handycam. She remarried into the socio-economic strata she'd been born in and can be found in central Jersey whenever she's not vacationing in Europe.

Ava survived her back-and-forth childhood and grew into a clever and creative girl with a penchant for foot-stomping tantrums. College seemed mostly an excuse to party, and no profession seemed to interest her. She pursued filmmaking by marrying it. Her young husband is a movie gaffer with DP ambitions, and Ava, now 24, is the mother of my six-month-old grandson.

Paul and Siri raised their daughter Sophie, a talented singer and actress, and their adopted son Ethan, a bright kid now in art school as a sculptor. Ethan has spent every summer since he was fourteen as my apprentice, laboring like a journeyman. While Siri continues to get traditional publishing contracts, Paul has become an expert self-publisher, putting his novels out on his own imprint via Amazon. He retired from the news business. They live in uptown Kingston, in the old Stockade District that once held a grip on my imagination.

I left filmmaking behind. I saw that my young self had chosen a career born of fear. It had kept me always one step removed from direct experience: life through a viewfinder, framed in an artificial rectangle. Life mediated. Observed, not fully lived. Surely this was entangled with the root causes of my misfortunes. Yet it's also true that my inner observer may have saved me.

As the world slid into everything digital, I learned that I am happiest as an analog man, preferring solid objects over the emptiness of ones-and-zeroes. For twenty years now I have been constructing beautiful and functional stone walls wherever such walls are needed. I occasionally build with mortar, but my reputation is for drystack walling, using native bluestone quarried right here in the Catskills. Bluestone is a fine-grained sandstone—or feldspathic graywacke to be precise—that is much harder and more durable than the red sandstone of the Utah desert. It was deposited as sediment in the Devonian period 380 million years ago, the sandy grains fused rock-solid under eons of unimaginable pressure. It forms the bones, the skeleton, of these mountains. And because it can be split into smooth, flat, bluish-gray slabs, it was once the material of choice for the sidewalks of New York City.

Building stone walls has its similarities to editing film or video: each shot, or each stone, must be selected and placed according to how its surface, or image/sound/emotion, meets the surfaces of the adjacent shots or stones. One at a time, each following each, they stack up to create a thing that is more than the sum of its parts. But there the similarity ends. In film and video, it's all mental. The content, the continuity, the story—none of those exist outside the viewer's mind. They're all part of the edifice of illusion we humans conjure like a misty garment around ourselves. But a wall is real, a solid thing forming a firm boundary. It is a dependable object in the physical world. And it will remain when I, the builder, am gone.

So I have packed another identity into my bag: Rose Stone, LLC. I love this work. My hands are rough and tired but my muscles are solid, my breath unhindered. I'll keep doing it until my strength gives out.

At the same time, my regular meditation schedule—resumed gradually with the birth of spring six months after my ordeal, and carried on until today—grounds me deep in the stratum of the silent void that is the wellspring of this illusory circus we call the world. I choose to keep practicing without seeking, my own slant on a favorite Nisargadatta quote: "There is nothing to practice. To know yourself, be yourself. To be yourself, stop imagining yourself to be this or that. Just be. Let your true nature emerge. Don't disturb your mind with seeking."

Every two weeks for a decade I had dinner with my artist friend Ted in a cozy little nook in his house. We talked about everything, and sometimes I could swear I felt my DNA changing. Perhaps I was ready when it was his time to go. He died in his studio at the age of 89.

I found it fascinating that the more time I spent with Ted,

and the more I looked at his paintings, I began to observe in the photos HueyMac sent me of his own work, a growing similarity in form, tone, composition, to Ted's work. I never mentioned this to Hugh, even when we got together for our occasional coast-to-coast weekends. His daughter now lives near me, after her graduation from the Culinary Institute just across the Hudson.

*

In 2002 I married Gwen, a family therapist who is a decade my junior, and we built our simple little home in Willow. Much of it we did ourselves, laboring side by side, learning how to build as we built. She is capable and calm, a hard worker with more willingness to tackle unknown challenges than I have ever had. She is an observer and listener who thinks before she speaks. I learn from her every day.

I met Gwen on the auspicious occasion of New Year's Eve, 1999. We were each alone at a small dinner party at the home of a Woodstock client for whom I'd built a retaining wall and with whom I shared bits of common background. He was a photographer, CJ Angus.

"Ben, Gwen. Gwen, Ben," CJ said. We smiled, shook hands, and began a conversation that didn't stop until we kissed at midnight. I discovered with surprise that I was thrilled to speak with a woman whose eyes were at the same height as mine. But of course there was much more to it than that. Both in recovery from broken marriages, we called ourselves "just friends" for several months, until the magnetic force of attracted bodies brought us irresistibly to bed.

In the beginning, our favorite full-day date was to ride the bus down to New York City and stroll different neighborhoods, filling each other in on our pasts there. Gradually, the frequency of those day trips diminished to almost zero. She feels the same as I do. Every time I go to the city now, I am assaulted by crowds of ghosts rising up around me, both imagined specters from the Revolutionary War, and unbidden memories, apparitions from previous periods of my life. And most disorienting of all, by an overlay of the two, like a photographic double exposure that leaves me swimming in a figure-ground bewilderment. Today our favorite dates are hikes in the wild Catskills.

Gwen's first marriage had ended in part because of her "idiopathic infertility," meaning doctors just don't know. But we wanted to experience parenthood together, so we chose adoption. When we travelled to India to pick up our daughter, I made sure we visited the Mumbai neighborhoods that Lester Spanda had once mentioned to me. There it was on Khetwadi 10th Lane: the attic where Nisargadatta Maharaj had taught his followers. I don't count myself a devotee of him nor of any guru, but it was those teachings that I had carried around inside me all those years that turned my thoughts toward India when Gwen and I began to contemplate adoption. Our daughter Chandra is now a vivacious ten-year-old who loves rollerskating, which of course is what brought me to find the portentous videotape where images of NN slyly hid—the "accidental" discovery on this very coincidental date—the event that kicked this narrative off. In the end, the tape itself means nothing more than that, and so perhaps this narrative comes full circle. But not quite.

*

To me, it all means this: something is at work behind the scenes to order the world. The truth is encrypted without a key and written in invisible ink between the lines of this giant book of fiction. We walk everyday through a scripted drama, contrived to be literary. A street address that mirrors history, events that echo across centuries, dreams that tell the future, elusive assassins and hidden rooms, videos and photos found at particular places or on particular dates, improbable patterns of names, the orchestrated clockwork of decades: 1975, 1995, 2015, and my ages: 20, 40, 60. What will happen in 2035 when I am 80? Is that when I will face my death?

Connections and relationships between things, events, people, ideas.... Everywhere, if only we have eyes to see, are invisible lines of energy, weblike, making life a rich feast of... of what? There seems to be no meaning attached to this, yet it is true.

Or maybe it is only true for me. I am humbled and dazzled by the mystery.

Not long ago I saw the movie *Slumdog Millionaire*, which ended with a question: *Jamal Malik is one question away from winning 20 million rupees. How did he do it? A. He cheated, B. He's lucky, C. He's a genius, D. It is written.*

The movie's answer: D. That makes sense to me, but then comes the necessary question: Written by whom? To that question, there is no answer.

In the not-knowing, we must abide.

32: TODAY

At the mortuary this morning, I stared at the body of a man whose identity I assumed that I knew, even while knowing I knew very little. Of course, he was the lovable town vagrant who gave away calligraphy on stones. That's who I saw.

"So why are you showing me his body?" I asked Paul.

"Assumptions make us blind, my friend," he said, as he handed me a New York driver's license. The picture showed a younger, slightly less hirsute version of the man on the table. The name on the license was Dunne, Morgan David.

I stared at the license, dumbstruck.

"Morgan David, like Mogen David, the wine known as Mad Dog," said Paul.

I moved close to the table and took a long look at the immobile face. Now, beneath the gray whiskers and the wrinkles, I began to see him: the round, once-boyish face, the small nose. Dark blond strands were mixed with the dull gray hair that hung to his shoulders. His hands were still meaty, so recently capable of that familiar strong grip.

"Mad Dog Dunne," I said low, as if he could hear. "Lester. You crafty son of a bitch."

Was it possible he had assigned himself to be my anonymous guardian angel, watching over me and my family here in Woodstock for years now? A deranged mercenary killer taking a path of redemption? Finally finding his devotional heart? The thought brought sudden tears to my eyes.

Events of the past reeled out in my memory, lined up, and re-shuffled themselves. Everything looked different.

The murky images of the killing from my long-gone camera were suddenly forefront in my mind, recalled with all the clarity that was ever there. I knew I could dig into my old archives for my backups of that footage, but I didn't need to; I could see it. And I could see how my assumption had made me blind. NN had left the frame just before the pistol was heard. There was no evidence he had done the shooting. He could just as easily have been the one who was shot.

And, by extension, it wasn't Spanda's body in the burned car (my car, of course), it was NN's. Nilsson/Nachtmann/Nixon, the alliterating assassin whose every false name contained a negation, whose chameleon essence was ungraspable. A phantom who now seemed almost to have never existed at all.

I turned to Paul, who gave a nod and a look that told me he knew what I was thinking. But he was ahead of me.

"I called the Kingston Police Department while you were on your way here. As far as we knew, that body in the car was never positively identified, right? But we assumed it was Spanda, so I thought they might be interested in our dead friend here."

"You spoke to what's-his-name... Peluso?"

"No, he retired years ago and moved to Florida, but I was able to get a detective on the line. Young guy though, not there in '95. I described the case to him and he looked into his database, the cold case files. Here's the weird part: there is no such case in their records."

"Really. A whole homicide case doesn't just get lost under the sofa or something, right? So... either somebody had the records expunged, or you and I were in the grip of a mutual hallucination."

Paul gave a slow nod, looking at the floor as if for clues. Then he looked up at me. "Anything's possible."

"So it is."

It was going to take some time to digest all this, to look

at the past through a new lens. Paul and I chatted for a bit and agreed to get together again in a few days and talk about it. We spoke with the mortician and learned the process by which we could make a donation to cover Dunne's burial in the Woodstock Artist's Cemetery. "Morgie," eccentric calligrapher of the streets, would get a lovely final resting place. No one need ever know what we knew.

Back at home, I paced the deck, my mind racing. The more I thought about it, the more I realized there were now more questions than answers.

I looked up the phone number of the Ponckhockie Union Congregational Church. To my surprise, I connected right away with the current pastor of the church, whose congregation, he said, had shrunk to the point that he did everything himself. His voice was gentle, a practiced kindness.

"Fourteen years I've been here," he told me. "I didn't really know my predecessor, but I've learned pretty much everything about this building and its history."

"Do you remember in the nineties, the news story about the caretaker of your church, who claimed he had assassinated Yasser Arafat?" I didn't want to reveal my own involvement in the creation of that story.

"Hmm, can't say I do. Sounds pretty ridiculous though, doesn't it?"

"He lived in the little apartment at the back of the church, but then he went missing."

"Apartment? What apartment?"

"You know, the back door, under the stairs, the little apartment there."

"You must be mistaken. That door leads to a storage area and the boiler room. There's never been an apartment there. I don't even think we ever had a caretaker, for that matter. Building maintenance is usually a joint effort by our parishioners, an act of service."

I was both alarmed and beginning to grow accustomed to such surprises. "But I was actually there—"

He cut me off. "I don't mean to be contrary, sir, but perhaps it was another church? You know, twenty years is a long time and...." He trailed off, suggesting the conversation was over due to my faulty memory. Maybe he was right.

"Thanks for your time," I said, and hung up.

That's when I came out onto the deck to sit in the perfect autumn air, to meditate, to watch the leaves drift down and the shadows drift imperceptibly across the lawn.

The light is in motion; we know that with certainty. The day proceeds. Yet in each of its moments the shadows appear to lie perfectly still. Two truths, opposing and simultaneous. All of this, this story like a great river running through me, undeniable in my memory, and yet... what is real?

I have the option, of course, to pursue the so-called "truth." To chase down Peluso and the cold case, to find the John Doe grave, to go to the church and see the "storage room" for myself, to research the "real" Mad Dog Dunne. But I choose not to. Those old stories are little more than remembered dreams; they are not current reality. They are irrelevant. I have had two decades of growth to internalize the lesson that the specter of Death, NN in all his forms, will either take me or he won't. Whether I fear him or not makes no difference, so I choose no fear.

I choose no fear even in the face of this one last thing that happened as the day drew to its end.

"Chandra," I called, "Want to come with me to walk Max?"

"No, I'm watching your skating videos," she said through her closed bedroom door.

Gwen, in her time-off tank-top and comfy shorts, was standing barefoot at the kitchen counter chopping vegetables. "Don't be long," she said. Her tawny hair was in a loose bun, a few stray strands drifting toward her pale shoulders. I came up behind her, put my hands on her waist and kissed the back of her neck. She put down the knife, turned, put her arms around my neck and pressed her entire slender but plentiful self against me with a full-on lustful kiss.

"Is that a promise?" I said.

"No, it's a command." She smiled and went back to cutting.

As I walked our scruffy little mutt up the forest-lined road in the growing dusk, I passed a nearby home that had recently been on the market, and saw that the For Sale sign was gone, lights were on, and a man was getting out of a car in the driveway. He was fiftyish, short and stout with a few strands of pale orange hair and round glasses above his ruddy cheeks. He gave a wide smile and a wave.

"Howdy neighbor! I'm the new kid on the block."

"Welcome to the neighborhood." I approached and shook his hand. "Ben Rose. I'm two lots down—over there."

"Oh! You're the stone wall man that was recommended to me. Very pleased to meet ya!" He spoke with an accent that took me a moment to place: he was Irish. "I need some wall work—y'know, add some definition to this overgrown yard. I like clear boundaries. Put a frame on it, y'might say."

"I can certainly help with that."

"I've had this thing about boundaries ever since, y'know, the Troubles. Back home."

"Oh... right, the Troubles." I thought this was probably none of my business.

He kept talking and smiling. "Gotta keep the lines clearly drawn, right? Damn right. We tried, tried and failed. Took plenty of the bastards down, though, didn't we, eh?"

I just nodded. He talked.

"Damn me, goin' on again. Not smart. Can't really chat about that, if y'know what I mean. Old history, danger. But... stone walls now, yes."

"Okay. Can we meet on Monday, talk it over?" Max was pulling the leash to resume our walk.

"Sure! I'll be here all day, just knock on the door."

"Will do." I turned back. "Oh—what's your name?"

With a sunny smile, he said, "Niall Noone. See you soon, Ben."

ABOUT THE AUTHOR

Brent Robison lives in the Catskill Mountains of New York with his wife, a maker of fabulous masks, and their wise-cracking teenage daughter. His fiction has appeared in over a dozen literary journals and several anthologies, and has won the *Literal Latte* Short Short Award, the *Chronogram* Short Fiction Contest, a Fiction Fellowship from the New Jersey Council on the Arts, and a Pushcart Prize nomination. His collection of linked short stories, *The Principle of Ultimate Indivisibility*, is available from booksellers everywhere. He blogs occasionally at Ultimate-Indivisibility.com, and co-hosts *The Strange Recital*, TheStrangeRecital.com, a podcast about fiction that questions the nature of reality. His second novel, now in progress, threatens to take him to the grave.

A REQUEST

If you enjoyed this book, its publishers and author would be grateful if you would post a short (or long) review on the website where you bought the book and/or on Goodreads.com or other book review sites. Thanks for reading!

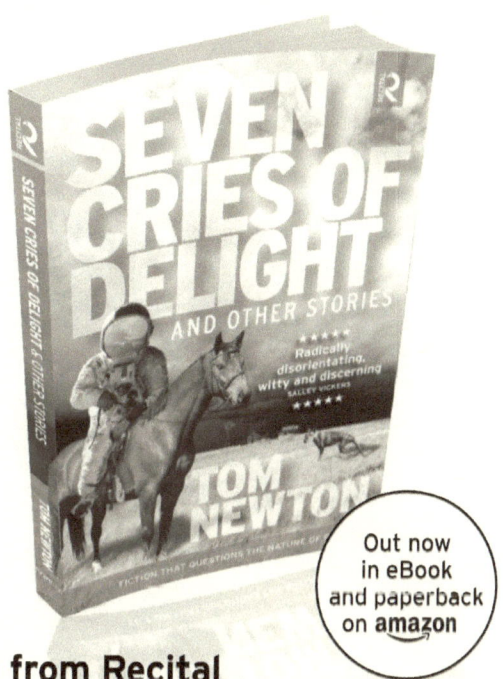